I0625971

The PRECIOUS QUEST

By Cheryl R Cowtan

Copyright © 2019 Cheryl R Cowtan

Cover design by Cheryl R Cowtan
using Canva.com
All rights reserved. If you wish to use brief quotations for media coverage, reviews or literary analysis, please use proper citation format and include my personal web site link at cherylcowtan.com[1]. This book may not be reproduced or distributed in any form without the author's permission. Thanks for understanding and supporting authors by complying with copyright laws.
Written in Canada.
eBook ISBN 9780978088965
Print ISBN 9780978088958
Please visit the author at
http://www.cherylcowtan.com

Oath
Upon the goddess-light, I swear all characters within this text are as ethereal as the mist upon the hill-sands. They exist only as figments of my imagination and do not represent any person, real, alive or dead. Names of locations and my efforts to create an imaginary world are used in a fictitious manner, and are not meant to represent the company, actual setting, or current physical business practices of any property or person.

---

1. http://www.cherylcowtan.com

This book is dedicated
to all those who
dream of days when
swords and scabbards
weighed heavy upon
the hip, and honour
was King.

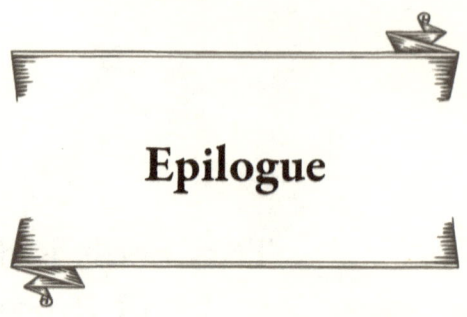

Epilogue

L ife was once understood through the cycle. We warred, we died, and we were reborn. New life was a gift from the goddess. It had been this way since the beginning. Then, without warning, there were no more gifts. The only way to have a child was to steal one, and eventually, there were none left to steal.

My people have not borne a child in nineteen years. Searching for answers, we have traveled far out of our domains. Further even than our Chronicle Warden's memory can trace. Every colony, every tribe we come to is childless. The cycle for them, as for us has stopped. Many of my people have accepted their fate, few will question the goddess' will, and fewer still will act.

But I am Laywren, Queen of the Horde. And I do not accept extinction as my destiny.

Chapter 1: The Decline of Doubt

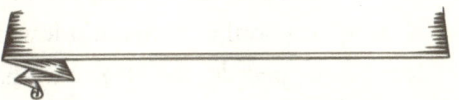

The giant opened his blood-stained hand and released the over-sized axe. It fell slowly, twisting from his great height to swoop like a sickle before striking a rock. The clang was like a too-late warning in the after-battle silence, but it caught my attention in time for me to witness my mighty warrior dropping forward onto his knees.

No sooner had his impact forced clouds of red dust to billow around his massive thighs, then I had nocked an arrow and panned the deadly point across the forest at his back. Yellow leaves flickered deceptively in the wood, but I held steady, staring at the black trunks of the trees until my eyes watered.

The giant, Nethaz, lowered his head, his long black hair sliding like silk away from his pale neck. In the distance between us, the bodies of our enemies lay twisted on the battlefield. They were no longer a threat and no opponent stepped out from the forest to challenge our victory.

I released the tension in the bowstring and in my shoulders, confused by the giant's sudden fall. He tipped forward onto one hand, the other clenching his stomach.

"What ails you?" I called out.

"Waste..." The word tore from this throat like a gag, and his powerful torso arched against his leather chest straps.

A deep throb kicked up in my temple counting out the seconds as I stepped cautiously closer. Finally, the heaving in his guts subsided and he sat back on his haunches and raised his face to the sky.

The agony in his features was too much for me.

"You claim this offering to the goddess as wasteful?" I gestured to the bodies.

"Death!" he roared, "Can you not see the death?"

"See it?" I shouted with pride. "I brought it!"

A long, keening moan escaped his twisted mouth releasing a deep regret that rippled through my soul with insult. How dare he regret the days of battle, the loss of our people, the efforts we had gone through to serve the goddess in our warring.

I wanted to strike him about the head until he bled from the ears.

"We are victorious!" I marched the final feet across the bodies of our slain enemies, shouting as I went. "We, the Horde, who live and fight in the service of the goddess, brought death to those who would defy her."

His shoulders shuddered as he grieved like an old man at the end of a wasted life. Disbelief chilled me to a stop. To mourn our service was dishonour. But worse, the giant's tears were a scourge, a plague that could only bring unrest to the warriors of the Horde and challenge to me as their ruler. I resisted the urge to cast my eyes Hallward for fear the goddess would meet my gaze and witness my shame.

An overwhelming need to strangle Nethaz's next moan before it left his lips struck me into action. Turning my bow his way, I aimed the sharp-edged arrowhead at his white-skinned chest.

"Laywren." A calm voice from behind tugged at my death-stare.

Dorn, my advisor, stepped into my side-vision and looked from me to Nethaz and back to my bow. "What would you do?"

I kept my eyes on the giant. "Step back, Warden, and allow me to sweeten the air with silence."

A quiver started deep within my elbow as the bowstring begged for release. My face burned with disgrace as I allowed another sob to escape the giant's lips and take to the sky.

"Would you slaughter one who has just fought for your glory?" I could feel Dorn's eyes searching for mine.

"There is no glory in weakness."

I started to unbend the calloused creases of my fingers and slowly released my breath as the giant drew his last.

Dorn stepped between me and Nethaz, his strong chest boldly framing the arrowhead.

I tried to re-hook the tension, but it was too late. The bowstring zinged the tips of my bending fingers. I jerked the bow in the hope of changing the arrow's path as a cry of frustration tore from my mouth. The feathers ripped the skin between my fingers, and Dorn twisted his upper body to the left, too slow to avoid the deadly dart. Yet, the arrow missed its mark and blurred into the forest ahead.

"Fool!"

My heart pounded against his reckless insolence and how close I had come to losing him. Dorn gave me a light bow, then turned and walked to the giant.

This time I did cast my eyes Hallward, for I know a flying arrow is true to its path once released...unless a divine hand changes its course.

Flipping his red cape back over his shoulder, Dorn bent to gaze into Nethaz's contorted face. A shuddering sob burst from the giant's trembling mouth to blow Dorn's light brown locks away from his brow. Placing his hand on Nethaz's wide shoulder, Dorn spoke soft words, a soothing spell. But the giant did not respond.

As I drew closer to them, I looked to the spattering of dusty, red soil sprinkled on the giant's white thighs like spice. It coated the toes of Dorn's boots and reminded me of the goddess' impending disfavour. We were standing on ground that would not grow food, nor hold water. We did not need any more misfortune.

As was Dorn's way, he stood and stared across the battlefield, giving his decision much thought. He held more knowledge than any living person in the Horde. He was the Chronicle Warden, the storyteller, the keeper of our legends and our past. His word was revered, and I always sought advice from Dorn before I made my decisions. He was not a man to be dismissed, easily, as much as I wanted to rail at him for daring to interfere. My patience in waiting for his conclusion was almost spent when he finally turned his eyes my way. As was right, he waited for me to invite his opinion.

"Come closer, so I might judge your loyalty," I growled.

A smile played at the corners of his lips, his too-bold way of acknowledging my half-hearted disapproval.

I place my hand on my dagger and was rewarded by his slight hesitation as he approached. When he was standing close enough, I could see the flecks of black in the amber of his eyes, I nodded.

"Nethaz's heart bleeds for the slain."

"We do not bleed for the dead." I struck the clotted wound at my side. "We bleed for the living."

Dorn's face was grave. "Without him, we may not have turned the charge of District warriors."

I was aware of the giant's might. Nethaz had fought like a god, swinging his axe into the mass of enemies without fear of mortal wound. He had served the goddess well. But a warrior who breaks inside is useless in battle and cannot be trusted.

Dorn continued with a reassuring smile, "He will fight for you again."

My instinct was strong, and the training under my warlord father was rigid. A broken warrior should be dealt with like a lame horse. I knew this. But what was clear in the past, was no longer clear in the present, and my father was now part of my past. Dorn was here, living in this changed world with me, his glance searching my face for a sign I would relent.

"The arrow tracked left when it missed me, not right." Dorn broke into Chronicle rhythm as if he were retelling the tale back at camp. "It was a divine hand that pushed it from the giant's might."

I considered the idea that the arrow had missed the giant and not him. It was possible, though painful for me to admit how close I had come to displeasing the goddess if this were so—if the giant was goddess-blessed. There was no way to be sure, and one must always err on the side of the goddess' favour. Nethaz living another day would not incur her wrath as much as killing him if she still wished the giant to serve.

I slid my bow into the sheath on my back. The stretch cracked open the wound in my side with a sharp prick and blood tickled down onto my dusty thigh. We had begun the battle at dawn, and I was weary. Perhaps that is the true reason why I let Nethaz live, or perhaps I no longer could stomach guessing at the goddess' will.

Dorn continued his appeal, as if I were not yet convinced. "The giant's time with us has been short, but his loyalty is strong, Laywren."

I turned my back on him and began the long walk back to camp.

His strong legs brought him easily to my side, where he matched my stride. "I cannot explain his behaviour, but I perceive no threat to the Horde."

"You serve the past, Dorn, not the future."

"The past and the future are the same."

"Tell that to them," I waved at the field spread with dead and wounded warriors from Horde and District.

"Laywren," Dorn stopped walking and clasped my elbow.

I turned and glanced at the bronze circlets gripping his forearm. He dropped his hand from my arm, but the pained expression in his eyes held me still for his query.

"You do not question the cycle?"

In another place and time, to question the cycle would have meant death. Within the Horde, I was the law. I was the bringer of death, yet I could not answer. I could not give voice to my doubt. I knew the words would begin the final unraveling of our order, our codes, and our lives, just as Nethaz's tears would.

I WAS SAVED FROM HAVING to speak by a baying that split the thick air. Our wound-hounds broke from the far forest, racing toward the battlefield. Strong-shouldered beasts of grey fur with lolling tongues ran among the bodies, sniffing and seeking, needing to begin the curing. One sat, raised its muzzle to the sky and howled the death song for a master who could not be healed; then another. The mournful cries took my mind back to other battles, other wounds. So many times, I had been saved from injury, waste or disease by my hound's healing.

The pattering of his wide paws announced my wound-hound's arrival. With a whine, Hinfūs scented my spilled blood and leaned into my side. The oily smell of his fur mixed with the spicy scent of smoke that hung in the air. I squatted, draping my arm over my hound's neck, and squinted through the swirling haze hanging over the field closer to the District. Beneath the haze were the bodies. Members of the Horde moved with their heads down, collecting weapons from the dead. One warrior raised her arms and drove down a sword—a mercy stroke.

Beyond the hounds and the bodies, the barricade of sun-bleached, twisted wood that protected the District dwellings towered against the red-tinged sky. The branches of our enemies' living barrier were armed with thorns the length of my finger. It had turned out to be an impassable mass of twisted, wooden growth that our helve axes could not breach, that our fires could not burn. But we had set fire behind the wall and that had driven their warriors out to greet us.

They had swarmed, ready as bees from a battered hive; a mass of buzzing anger that forced us back into the field. The people were honey-coloured and wore armour emblazoned with a wild boar. We did not know their kind, did not know their deity or their ways, but we knew they had food and water. That had made them our target. Made them our mark still, for we had not been able to breach the wall. I was sure it was spelled with magicks, for the warriors who had come out through the thorny wood had not left an opening for us to move through.

Opening or no, we had to get in, for behind the twisted wall of branches would be something the goddess had denied the Horde. Young. Without born young, we could not replace those who had died today, or yesterday, or the thousands of days before that had not seen a child born to our people. To any people.

A familiar numbness threatened to clamp my limbs in iron. I knew Dorn would sense my despair and seek to sooth me. And so, I shook the memories away and hoped instead of the waiting children and the tinkling of their laughter. The echo filled my chest with warmth. Hinfūs' trusting glance took in my slight smile and set his bushy tail to thumping against the ground. I stood to avoid inhaling the rising dust.

A flash caught my eye by the District wall. The last rays of day winked as it reflected off a warrior's armour. From this distance, he seemed a man surrounded by a mystical glow, but I knew him as Rserker, my general. No other man would be so vain as to wear a golden chest-plate or so foolish in this heat.

I put two dirt-caked fingers into my mouth and whistled loudly. Rserker turned his head, and I raised my hand. Dorn waited quietly by my side as Rserker moved on powerful legs toward us. The soil barely stirred as he crossed it, for it was heavy with blood closer to the District. But as he neared, the red cloud that dogged all our movements rose to his knees.

I reached out my right hand and clasped the cool metal of armour below his elbow.

"Brother," I hailed him, pleased that he lived.

His strong hand wrapped my leather arm guard. "Sister," his deep voice returned my greeting as he pulled my arm against his chest.

"The Griffain will tire this night." Dorn praised the outcome of the battle.

Rserker released me and clapped his hand onto Dorn's shoulder. "May the souls' journey to the Hall be swift," he boomed.

"May their journey back be swifter," Dorn replied with a smile.

Although we nodded, the ancient saying did not ring true in my mind. I kept my doubt in the souls returning, my dishonour from my face.

"What did you hear behind the wall?" I asked Rserker.

"Silence," he said, his blue eyes shining with his strength of will. "But they are there. We will find our way through."

"And the age of the youngest warriors?"

"Young enough to cut their chins when they shave." He smiled at me, his teeth big and white against his sun-bronzed skin.

Swallowing against my parched throat, I nodded. These people had younger members than the Horde. Perhaps they could still bear young. It was enough for hope.

I licked my lips, tasting the soot at the corners of my mouth. "Continue with your search," I said to Rserker. "Seek beneath the armour of the younger women. Look for signs that any have carried a child."

Dorn sought to ease the desperation in my voice. "Look alive while you search lest the Griffain mistake you for the dead," he said to Rserker

"And carry me to the Hall?" Rserker scoffed and slapped his chest plate. "This beating heart is too heavy for their talons."

A thought struck me, a thought that drove my heart into my throat and made me speak without thought.

"If a live warrior could seek the Hall, we could learn why the door to return has been barred against us."

Dorn and Rserker stilled and it seemed as if the very smoke itself hung suspended in the air, at a loss without a wind. I had spoken rashly, but now the words were released, I was free to face my doubt in the souls' returning. I held my head high. Rserker bowed and backed away two steps before turning to walk toward those awaiting his command.

I dropped my eyes from his retreating form and spied a female warrior in the dirt. She wore leather breast armour as I did. I pushed her arm with my sandal. It resisted. The District warrior's body had begun to stiffen into the shape of the battle-fallen—the message to the Griffain that she belonged in the Hall of Return. I knelt and slit the ties on her body armour, moving it off to the side. Running my hand across her smooth stomach, I was disappointed to find no breaks in the fat beneath her skin, no lines from the stretch of child bearing. Her stomach was firm like mine. I sat back on my heels, rubbed my hand across my face and sighed.

"She is only one," Dorn said.

And there's the wound, I thought, as a pain started deep in my chest—the ache of the barren. The muscles in my arms and neck began to tighten as if my body would stiffen into the shape of a slain warrior as well. Perhaps, I was fallen. Perhaps the battle had been lost long before I had lifted my sword. I could not draw my gaze from the warrior's tight stomach, even as I felt my hound licking the wound in my side.

Dorn knelt beside me. "The Griffain come," he whispered.

His soft voice drew my mind from its pause. I looked up, noting the light had changed. It was near dark. Through the shadowy air, the trees surrounding the battlefield blurred into a grey smudge of soft-edged mounds. I held my gaze until I saw it. Movement in the trees—slight flickers of darkness among the north stand of forest. Griffains! Beasts of burden for the goddess. Their gripping talons and strong wings earned them the privilege of flying the dead to the Hall.

A bead of sweat trickled down the inside of my armour, cooling my skin and making me shiver. I stood and ignored the prickle in my legs from squatting so long. Across the field of dead, my warriors moved with torches, seeking the female fallen. The flickering of the flames created a false writhing among the still bodies. This trick of shadows and the rhythm of the warriors' song of life would ward off the Griffain for only a short time. I looked to the forest's edge where I had last seen Nethaz. The giant was gone. A Griffain shrieked with impatience.

"There is nothing more to be done here," Dorn said.

We turned to make our way back to camp. Hinfūs dogged my steps with ears down. I lightly pushed him away.

Dorn clasped his hands behind his back and asked, "Why do you think Nethaz grieved the death of our enemies?"

My voice, heavy with loss, revealed my thoughts. "Nethaz grieves the cycle."

"Without death, there is no life." Dorn spoke the words that were as ancient as the great trees in the forest.

Then, against all that I had been taught, I spoke the unthinkable, "There will be no life from this battle," I said. "There was no life from the last, nor the one before that."

"Laywren!" Dorn stopped walking. I hardened myself against his shock.

"Life has been denied us," I whispered harshly, and waited for the goddess to strike me down.

Chapter 2: A Visit from the Goddess

I had hidden behind a wooden fence, in the days when there was still enough wood to build with. Crouching low beneath my brown cloak, I had watched the refugees shuffling along the horse path on their way to our village. Even as a youth, I could see these were a defeated people, starving, broken, no hope left in their hearts. In the past year, more and more people had walked this way, leaving behind their homes, their lands, claiming that a drying wind was pushing its way over soil. This wind, they claimed, carried away the dirt needed for roots to take hold and so, plants, animals, people all fell in its wake.

In our village, we still had food though fresh vegetables and fruit were becoming scarcer as seasons had become warmer and plants had browned beneath the too-bright sun. Our main staples were meat from the animals who could forage in the dry grasses that became more brittle each year.

I was happy to see the trailing line of outsiders, for they were outcasts and foreign. A different people from a different place, and I hoped they would take the taunts that were usually cast my way.

My mother was also an outsider. She had been captured by my father and as a battle bride she was afforded a grudging acceptance out of respect to my father. But I was a half-breed, a product of a joining of two peoples. I was not fully one, nor fully the other, and therefore, less than every person in the village. Though I tried to be more, tried to win every race, every fight, be the strongest, the smartest, I was always reminded that I was less each day from the smallest child to the eldest leader in our clan.

I watched the struggling steps of the weary travelers until the line petered out and only an old woman dragged her rag-covered feet along. She wore a cloak much like mine, but hers opened at the front where the material was edged with feathers. It had been a fine cloak at one time, though now it was covered in dust and filth. Her face was shaded by the hood so far did its edges stand out, but long tendrils of white hair slipped from within the hood to tangle with the feathers along her concave chest.

She staggered over the ruts, first taking a step to the left and then one to the right, and I realized with this weaving advance, she would never catch up to the others. Suddenly, she stopped. Seeming confused, her shoulders slouched even more, and her gnarled fingers dropped her walking stick.

I cautiously looked around for the youngsters who took great sport in pelting me with stones. When assured they were probably closer to the village pelting the newcomers, I slipped silently from behind the fence. I darted on stealthy feet to clutch up the woman's walking stick, and then I danced a few feet away and stood between the old woman and the village.

I struck the ground with her stick, and said, "This is the way they have gone, old one."

Her head lifted beneath the hood and she shuffled her body to face me, but she did not speak.

"Come!" I repeated.

"Such a commanding voice for such a frail looking slip of a girl," a rasping voice filtered from the beneath the cloth.

I straightened my shoulders and adopted my imposing stare I used on the village bullies. "I am not so frail."

The old woman tucked her hands beneath her cloak. "You have much pride in your stance, child."

"I am not a child."

She cackled.

Angry that a stranger would mock me already, I barked, "Come! You must be with the others when the elders decide your fate."

"Must I?" She shuffled closer, and though I had intended to give her the staff, I found myself keeping the distance between us. "Who, but the goddess, has the right to decide my fate?"

My eyebrows went up and I asked, "You serve the goddess?" How strange it was to me to find this outsider served the same deity as we did. That was rare in these days of nomads. "How far have you come, old woman?"

"I have come a lifetime to find you."

Again, she stepped forward and I stepped back. Confused by her words, I was now sure she was addled in the brain as well as feeble. I wiped my nose with my arm as I considered what to do with her. Deciding that the longer I lingered, the higher my chances of being discovered speaking to an outsider and being punished would be. I had to either leave her, or get her moving in the right direction, and then scurry back into the shadows.

I moved closer; my hand outstretched. "You may lean on me."

When I grasped her arm beneath the cloak, I was surprised to feel muscle along her arm. A sudden flash of brilliance blinded my eyes, causing me to cry out and crouch, pulling her down with me. But in my hand, there was nothing. It was as if she had dissolved with the light and left me squatting on the horse path by myself.

When the spots cleared from my eyes, I stood warily. The walking stick seemed heavier in my grip, and I looked down astonished to see that I no longer held a wooden staff, but instead a burnished sword was gripped in my fist.

"Goddess!"

I dropped the weapon and leapt to the side, afraid it would slash me, or some evil befall me. It struck the ground and lay still. I cast my frightened glance around to ensure I was still alone, then looked at my hands which seemed to be betraying me by losing things and clutching changing objects.

The palms of my hands were dusted with a powdery red ochre. I brushed them together and watched the red dust rise and hang weightless in the air. It got into my nostrils and then into my lungs, and I sneezed.

That had been the first time I'd seen the red dust. I had not known then that it would blow across our lands and dry everything in its wake. I had not known then, that the dust was the enemy, the harbinger of death, the slayer of worlds.

I had also not known that before the dust would come, I would be cast out of the village, cast to wander in the wastelands like the old woman.

Only I would not be travelling alone, for I had learned one important thing from my lonely life in the village, and it was that all people under the goddess were worthy of belonging. And all people, under the goddess, were worthy of life. And so, my sword in hand, I had gathered the nomads who would pledge to me. And I pledged to the goddess that my mixed band of mixed breeds would find a way to survive in a dying land, even if we had to traverse the entire length of our world.

Chapter 3: The Warrior's Tale

The wall of twisted wood surrounding the District grew in the dirt like a birch reflects on the shore of a still lake—twenty feet up and seven feet down. We had tried and failed to breach it with brute strength. But the Horde had more than just force. We had patience and enough supplies to camp outside the wall for two weeks. So, after the battle, I placed sentinel pacers in the forest, and while they watched for movement from the District, my warriors healed their battle wounds.

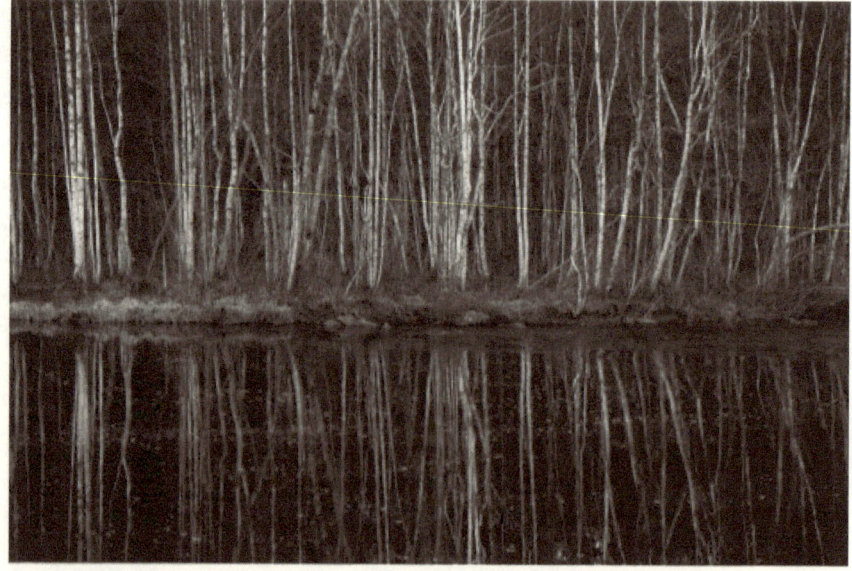

I had the time to consider Nethaz's behaviour after the battle. It was my General's responsibility to ensure the giant understood our ways. Three months before, the colossal man had appeared on the horizon. Surrounded by my warriors, he had pleaded to join the Horde. As was our tradition, Rserker had accepted the oversized warrior as wúsc-bearn or adopted one. As such, Rserker was to have ensure the giant's previous alliances, values and honour-bonds were forsaken. To be one of the Horde each member had to pledge their allegiance to me. The giant should have been prepared when he swore his allegiance and pledged his bohr-hand. And it seemed he was for he had fought well against the District warriors, but I was left uneasy by his reaction to our victory.

ON THE SECOND DAY AFTER the battle, I asked Nethaz to walk with me. The air was hot and dry, tightening my skin over my cheekbones with its harsh breath. The climate did not seem to bother Nethaz. His white skin lay thick above a layer of fat that softened his rippling muscles. He tossed his head back like a stallion, and his black hair glistened in the sun with the gloss of freshly applied grease. I was tall, but such was the giant's height that I walked one and a half paces to his every step. He slowed to match my speed.

Ahead of us, a high ridge protected the camp from the moisture-sucking winds. I chose that as our mark, for I wanted to look around while we were out. With a few quick bounds, I reached the first of the hardy brush roots, then used my hands to pull myself up the steep incline. Nethaz's grunts as he scrambled in the loose soil told me what I already knew, that our encampment would tire any enemy willing to climb the ridge on the canyon side.

Making the crest, I stood tall, controlling my breathing and turned to look down on the camp. From this height, the brown-skinned tents scattered in the dirt below looked like throwing bones in a warrior's game. It reminded me how vulnerable we were, living week to week on our rations, warring with others to replenish our food and water, travelling across dangerously inhabited lands.

Ringing the boundary of camp were our beasts of burden, their oversized heads hanging down until their wide nostrils skimmed the dirt. These witless creatures seemed slothful, but with the Julees in command, nothing could pass through the perimeter without a trumpeted warning and a stomping that would press the blood of any enemy like wine. Yes, the ridge gave us the best advantage, protecting our camp from view, from the worst of the winds, and beyond the tents the forest provided an escape.

Nethaz grabbed at a clump of dried grass by my feet, but it ripped loose, and he slid back 10 feet. The soft dirt buried his feet up to his thick ankles.

"Make haste, Giant," I said, flatly.

He continued to grunt and claw until he was able to drag his heavy body up to the edge. He didn't flop to the ground and pant like a dog but got to his feet as he should and stood to face my judgement.

"You dishonoured yourself on the battlefield."

Few men would have taken such an insult without drawing their blade. But he did not even drop his head in shame. His blue eyes remained steadily fixed on mine, unreadable and clear like the moist skies of my childhood.

Finally, he spoke. "The lives I took are my dishonour."

A muscle in my jaw jumped. "Your duty lies with the Horde and with your Queen!" In my anger, my hand had found the pommel of my sword. "You were fighting for both."

Nethaz slowly lowered his bulk to one knee, his head bowed before me. "I have pledged myself and my weapon to you, and I serve you as you command."

"Serving is not enough! You should not question my commands with mind nor heart."

A year ago, I would have slain him for his disgrace. But the goddess had spared his life from my arrow, and I was bound to only wield my tongue instead of my sword. I was also keenly aware of the falling numbers in the Horde. I had need of his axe.

I looked over Nethaz's head to the camp below and recalled my father's voice to guide me. Many times, my father had told me the "Tale of the Warrior's Task". This story had been part of my teaching, part of my molding as I had become the combatant I was. I decided Nethaz needed to hear it.

I touched the giant's shoulder, releasing him from his kneeling position. His skin was strangely cool in this heat and caused me to wipe my fingers against my thigh.

Taking a calming breath, I sat on the ridge, pulling my cloak beneath me. The brown-edged grasses pricked at my legs, while my pride prickled within. I taught lessons with the blade, not the word, but things were not as they once were. I crushed the sharp grasses down with my sandaled heel. When Nethaz had settled his bulk beside me, I spoke.

"As a warrior, you do not take lives on the battlefield; you release them to the goddess."

Nethaz pulled his legs up and wrapped his melon-sized knees with his muscular arms. His shoulder was on level with my eyes.

"It is your duty to fill the Hall with souls, so that they may return."

I opened the little leather bag at my side and took out my carving of the goddess. Years before, I had carved her from an Oil Berry tree. The wood shone smooth where my hands had worn her curves. Holding her snugly in my palm, my cracked skin cradled her like a babe. I began the tale as it had been told to me.

"Many lives ago, the world held many lives. And so, the fish, the birds, and the beasts became fewer in number, as people spread across the land in great numbers."

Nethaz nodded at my words.

"Goddess looked down with pride, for she was Mother of all the land. Yet she was also troubled, for she foresaw the fruits of the world could not be harvested by so many, for so long. And so, to protect those who were already born, the Mother decided she would birth no more broods."

I passed my goddess carving to Nethaz, and he took it gently in his large hand. The wood looked darker against his fairer skin.

"The mother also foresaw that some of her children must be taken from the world, so it could blossom for the others."

Nethaz trailed his thick thumb over her round belly.

"Yet, how could Goddess choose the way and the ones to remove from the world? No mother could."

"No," agreed Nethaz. His deep voice rumbled in my lungs. "No mother could."

Nethaz locked his fingers together, forming a woven basket of flesh. Then he raised his hands to his face and stared intently at the statue.

I paused as I thought of the woman who might have birthed this giant. Though his breadth was ample, that of three men, his features were not bulbous or crooked. His strong brow creased over a hatchet-sharp nose. And beneath, his lips were tinged with enough colour to define the edges which stood out sharply against his white skin. The giant was beautifully formed, much like the statues of the Tiberoon era. He was a fine example of the goddess' blessing, and yet I was still not sure he was of her.

"What mother could... And while Goddess toiled with the truth, the world gave forth less and less, and the children began to fight for what was left. The contests grew fierce, and many were slain."

Scooping up a handful of the baked soil, I sifted it through my fingers releasing the specks of powder to float in the hot air.

This is what's left, I thought.

At the sight of the dust moving in the air, my throat tightened so, I could hardly go on. There didn't seem to be a place we could escape the dust anymore. We travelled constantly, only stopping to make war, and still, we had not found an oasis within the distances we had traversed.

I stared down at the camp and wondered how I would ensure the survival of the Horde. The responsibility for my people was a constant weight upon my shoulders.

After some time, Nethaz cleared his throat, jarring me out of my pause. "They brawled over what was left, and many were slain," he prompted.

I sighed and then continued. "When our Mother saw her daughters and sons lying lifeless on the ground, she drew stars from the sky and turned them into fierce, white-winged creatures. She called them Griffain, and she sent them to fetch her dead babes back to her. The massive birds flew down to the world and scooped up the slain children in their talons, then carried them to the Hall among the stars. Though Goddess was saddened at the death of her children, she knew their inter-fighting had given her the answer to the world's survival."

I traced a circle in the red powder at our feet. "Our Mother cast the lifeblood of the slain and forged three rings. The first was the gift of birth which she gave to her daughters—the MÓdere."

I drew the second circle, linking it with the first, "The second was the gift of release, which she gave to her warring children—the DreÓdreng."

I dragged my finger in the dust. "The third was the gift of return."

My voice had become heavy, and it was here my wind died. I could not finish drawing the third ring, for the souls of my people had not returned.

Nethaz folded his knuckles over the goddess carving, blocking her from view. The wound in my side ached. I had set out to convince the giant of his duty, but I was no longer even sure of it myself.

His deep voice rumbled beside me. "The third ring, the gift of return, was given to her sons—the Firslain. They would guard the Hall and herd the souls, releasing one for every death to the world below."

I looked up at him in surprise. "Did Rserker tell you the tale?"

"They wait," he said.

"Who?"

"The souls. They wait in the Hall for their return."

I searched his eyes, and he held my gaze, clear and innocent with his thoughts.

"It is not the way to the Hall that has been barred, but the way back," he said.

I leaned closer until I could see the fine lines on his full lips.

"What do you know?"

His arched, black brows drew down over his eyes. "Those who serve the goddess serve themselves."

"You speak of the Firslain?" I asked, thinking of the elusive Priests of the Hall.

"The Hall is full, and the Firslain bar the way of return." He rubbed his white knuckles as though they were dirty.

My heat leapt in my chest. The giant was speaking heresy, endangering us all. But had I not been sharing my doubts? Was I not as guilty?

"How do you know this?"

He was still, his eyes glazed as if in a trance, but his hands continued to twist.

"Nethaz?"

I was worried his grip might crush my goddess carving, so I leaned over his thigh and placed my hand on his. My skin looked like grey stone upon his marble-lush hand, which stilled beneath my touch.

Without speaking, I pried opened his sausage-sized fingers, one at a time. He watched my hands rearranging his until the carving was revealed. I gently lifted the goddess from him and packed her safely away in my pouch. Nethaz continued to stare at his empty palm.

I considered his claim. The Firslain were highly respected—they were the instruments of the goddess, her own children. I could not fathom they would deceive her. To think such was blasphemy and set my skin to sweating.

Yet the souls had stopped returning, as if they were barred.

A cry from below tore me from my thoughts. I stood and looked down the ridge to see a man scrambling up the shifting sands like a dog on all fours.

"The sentinel pacer has returned," he shouted. "There is movement from the District."

The hot wind flipped the end of my cloak near Nethaz's face. He didn't flinch. I yelled down orders to have my advisors meet me in my tent to plan our next move.

Nethaz was still staring into space like a soulless one when I left him on the ridge.

Chapter 4: The District Hæsel Bush

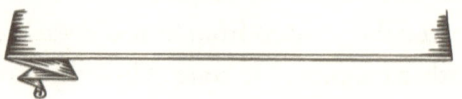

The flanks stood like sentinels at my tent, until they sensed me. Then they turned to watch my approach, their long jaws lazily grinding the region's grasses between their wide, flat teeth. They looked more like goats when they did that, upright goats with not a care in the world. Their slow movements gave the impression of slothfulness, but that was what made them excellent protectors.

My father had taught me it was better that an enemy dare and is revealed, than that he slinks unknown. Surely, one seeing the flanks chewing their cud would dare, but within seconds they could turn and then, woe to he who would attempt to pass them.

I jogged the last few feet, and the flanks straightened out of their slouching stance, becoming alert as they sensed the distress I felt at the giant's revelations. I assured them all was well, before passing through a haze of their musky odor to enter my tent.

Minutes later, the flanks allowed General Rserker to pass. His blonde hair and beard reddened in the sun's blush before he stepped into the dim interior. I crinkled the skin around my eyes in welcome. Rserker smiled boldly at me, his strong, white teeth as much a sign of his courage as his conquests. We had fought many battles together, and his pledge to me was unquestionable. He was my warrior kin—my war brother.

Dorn's long, sure strides brought him into the tent with a flourish. Had I not seen him enter, I still would have felt the charge in the air. Dorn could silence a crowd, drawing all attention his way. It was the manner of Chronicle Wardens. And it was a skill that could be used to take over a rule, but Dorn would never desire to lead. He only desired to record the leading, and then retell it.

Dorn's wise eyes glanced at mine to read my mood. He was always impatient to know how my emotions stood. He bowed deeply before me. His wavy, brown hair slipped forward to hang seconds before he straightened and tossed it back.

"Laywren."

Dorn spoke my name like he spoke the tales of our ancestors—with music. But today, he was not charming, not intent on teasing or flattering me. His forehead was furrowed with worry. He knew as well as I, that we needed to breach the District soon, and he was eager to hear any news.

"Welcome, Dorn."

I motioned for them both to sit.

As I lowered myself to the floor hides, my leather armour creaked like a fine saddle. The pacer arrived to report what she had seen at the District, but she stayed near the far wall. Her muscles were long beneath her skin, which was mottled with three shades of brown. She had been a Rainling, but now, she was part of the Horde. In the forest, she blended into the trees making her a stealthy watcher, and that is how I allowed her to serve.

I raised my war-calloused hand and commanded her to speak of the District wall and what she had seen.

She stepped forward to stand in the amber rays leaking through the air hole in the top of the tent. Squatting, she gracefully lowered herself to the floor. The pacer opened her mouth and sound came a second later.

"Twisted and immovable—the wood—like a washerwoman's knuckles. Slyness—the movement—like a rustling within the twigs. My ear it captured. Ten times, I breathed over the groaning; great trunks rubbing in the wind. But there was no wind. Straightening and pushing down—the curled wood—like planting sticks into the dirt."

Rserker was frowning as he listened to her raspy voice. The pacers were fast runners and silent watchers, but their speech was difficult.

"On hawrss back—men and women—rode out of the branches, into the forest."

"How many?" Rserker asked.

"Seven." The pacer curled her dusty fingers around each other.

"What happened to the wood after the riders passed?" Dorn asked her.

"Closing behind and around—the knots—springing after the last rider."

So, the wall was closed to us, again. I turned to Dorn who was leaning forward, intently considering the pacer's words. "Have you found a chronicle of the winding wood?" I asked him.

He turned his hands palm up, observing the lines in the creases of his fingers as he spoke, "I have delved deep within my memory, and I cannot find a tale of such a bush."

A Chronicle Warden could store many centuries worth of knowledge, but without access to such knowledge, what was the need for such a skill? My disappointment was great, but I kept silent to spare him from knowing.

"I do have a chronicle about a curling wood that will douse for water," Dorn turned to me. "It is Hæsel."

"Hæsel," I thought for a moment. "What shape does this Hæsel take when it douses?" I asked him.

"It is straight and forked as it yearns for the water, pressing down against the hand that holds it."

"This is a rain-forsaken place," Rserker winked at the sentinel pacer. "I too would dip my branches into the soil for a drink of fresh water."

The pacer did not look at Rserker—her timid eyes sought the sky through the tent's roof.

Tucking Dorn's story of the dowsing wood away for another day, I rose. The others stood.

"Rserker, send out a group to track and capture those who left the District. Gather everything you find about them. We must know all to determine the way through the wall."

Rserker struck his fist against his chest and swept out of the tent. I nodded at the pacer, releasing her. She slipped away, silent as a moth.

I moved to stand in front of Dorn. We were of the same height, but today Dorn's back was not strong. It bent under the weight of being an advisor with no advice. I sought his gaze, but his eyes were empty. His thoughts were inside, creating a new chronicle.

I waited while he stored the meeting in his mind, taking the chance to look over his features. In his amber eyes, I found the dark brown flecks, right where I knew they would be. Daughter of a Mantie mother, the sun had burned my skin grey, but Dorn was a light, golden tan. The grit of the region was buried deep in his pores, lining the creases where his smile would dimple. I checked his eyes to make sure he did not observe me, and then I dropped my glance to his lips. They were firm and full, the top line ridging beneath nostrils winging for the air to fill his legends.

"LAYWREN," DORN'S SOFT voice held a warm invitation.

I knew better than to meet his eyes. I had seen them burn before, and I could not chance drowning in their heat. I stepped back.

"What will you call the wood?" My question was meant to move us away from the moment, but when he answered, his voice was heady and low.

"Is that what you really want to ask me?"

"It is what I have asked you."

"Pig's tail Hæsel."

Each 's' in his answer was drawn out like a caress. He had to leave. I walked to the slit of the tent and waited. Dorn tilted his head in respect and joined me by the tent's entrance. He paused and looked out into the grey of first night. I studied his profile, and he knew it. Then, without a word he walked away.

A smile tempted my lips, but I held them straight and moved to stand between the flanks. The night air was filled with the sounds of voices speaking together, bursts of laughter, fire crackling, and animals snorting and pawing the ground. This song of life belonged to the Horde and filled me with a sense of wellbeing.

I slid my hand behind my chest armour and pulled out my medallion, Lumen. It hung on a leather cord around my neck, and it was directly connected to every person in the Horde. I had shut Lumen down for the battle for the disc opened a straight path into my mind, and I did not know what talents were hiding behind the District walls.

I spit on the disc and rubbed my arm in circles over it until it shone free of the grease of my breasts. The smooth surface caught the last light of day and reflected my face back to me. My skin, which had once been the colour of river stone, was turning to the dark grey of mountain slate under a sun that kept burning hotter each day. Each year, I felt more charred. My face, once sharp and dangerous, was now dulled by the red dust and heat into a map of our journey, drawn with lines of fatigue and water-loss. My cheekbones looked like jutting ridges under my heavy-lidded eyes.

But my eyes were still bright, glittering back at the smooth circle of my medallion with an unquestionable strength of will. My eyes, the colour of jungle violets, Dorn had said. Maybe the only jungle violets left in this world. The colour, so rare, it could grasp another with wonder and encourage village fools to want to beat the difference from me.

Now wonder had turned to fear. I had seen it in the eyes of my enemies as they took in the thick, dirt-matted braids that cascaded from my skull like a living headdress. My hair had been coated in red dust for so long, I no longer knew its true colour. It had become my battle-cap, fitting for a warrior who had released a thousand souls at the edge of her sword.

I ran my thumb over the raised runes around the edge of the disc, and a faint glow started up in the heart, erasing my reflection. Through Lumen, the flanks could now feel the quickening of my pulse, and I could feel Dorn's. I laid the medallion back on my chest above my armour-covered heart and relaxed against the familiar tug deep within my skull.

Sending out a gentle seek through Lumen, I counted the living recognizing each presence within the Horde. Many were no longer joined to me, and my awareness of the fallen deepened.

These lost warriors had fought by my side, under my command. Their gift should be a return, a new chance at life, but without babes their souls had no vessels to fill. And without souls, no babes would quicken.

Nethaz had said the Firslain, sons of the goddess, had locked the souls in the Hall. Every fiber of my being wanted to deny such a betrayal of son against mother. But I was surrounded by the proof that the souls were not returning. And what I could believe was that someone or something was preventing them.

How had we come to this?

Life had always been understood through the cycle. We warred, we died, and we were reborn. New life was a gift from the goddess. It had been this way since the beginning. Then, without warning, there were no more gifts. The only way to have a child was to steal one, and eventually, there were none left to steal.

My people had not borne a child in nineteen years. We traveled far out of our domains searching for one. Further even than our Chronicle Warden's memory can now trace. Every colony, every tribe we had come to was childless. And, now I would know if the District was as well.

A disharmony of faith haunted me, for my newly slain warriors were lost. I had to find a way to ensure their homecoming. I still hoped the people behind the magicked wall of Hæsel would have answers.

I felt there might be a clue in this Pig's Tail Hæsel wood of Dorn's, for surely anything that could find water in this thirsty world would be a blessing from the goddess.

I turned to Left Flank. "How do you straighten the tail of a pig?" I asked.

It continued to chew the grain-tipped grass drooping from its whiskered lips. Its pale eyes slid to Right Flank. They clicked and clattered—high pitched sounds chirping past the cud in their mouths. Lumen fed the translation directly into my mind.

Left Flank ~ Bore the boar ~

Right Flank ~ Bog the hog ~

Left Flank ~ Ring the rump ~

Right Flank ~ Hang the ham ~

The flanks were amused, but I considered their answers carefully. We had "bored the boar" by out-waiting the District, and now, foolishly, a group had fled. A group Rserker would soon overcome. Dorn had said Hæsel would dip for water and bogs were wet.

While I pondered the flank's riddles, Rserker and his men rode down the seven who had left through the District wall.

Chapter 5: The Tongue Holds the Key

The next night, dusk came in pink, tinting the dry grass until it seemed to flame above the soil. The flanks and I were positioned at the outer ring of tents waiting for Rserker's return. My guards stood back-to-back, watching the ridge and the forest at the same time. As the sun dipped down past the horizon, the slight drop in heat that marks the coming of night cooled my skin. Finally, out of the dim light, Rserker and his group arrived at the edge of camp leading the captives.

MY MEN ADOPTED A MORE relaxed posture once they were safely inside the camp's boundary. The seven who had escaped the District were resting awkwardly against their wrist and ankle bindings. The stillness of one was death. Of the living, three were women. Their small stature, dark brown skin and primitive clothing allied all of them, male and female, to the same tribe.

But, there was one who was different. Not different because of how he looked, but because of how the others were in his presence. Some were turned to the left and some turned to the right, but they all faced this one man. He was their leader. He was the one I wanted.

I raised my hood to hide my face and sent the flanks forward. Their long, goat-like legs carried them swiftly to the group. The captives flinched away from their thudding hooves, but the flanks ignored them. They moved to the leader and pulled him roughly into a standing position. The man did not struggle. Rserker sighted me, but I raised my hand, and he understood to stay with the other captives.

I turned and moved quickly through camp, followed by the flanks as they half dragged the biddable captive to my tent. I held up the door skin and they bent, their boney spines hackling their back hair as they slipped through. Left Flank stepped on the man's leg and made no rush to get off it. They were rough as they bound him to the thick, mid-pole.

Through all of this mishandling, the captive made no protest, and I made no move to stop the wrenching of his arms. When the flanks were sure he could not get free, they moved past me to guard the tent from the outside.

Hinfūs growled low, stalking towards us from the shadows of the tent's back wall. The captive's eyes rolled white in fear as he tried to twist on the pole to see what was coming up behind him.

Cradled within my hood, I waited quietly while I observed him. I was watchful for he had not struggled nor tried to communicate when we had tied him. I did not assume he was a coward or accepting of his fate. To believe so would be to let my guard down and that could be perilous, especially if he had magicks.

It was hard to know if he held certain powers by how he looked. I was not familiar with his kind or their dress, but I could see his hair had been done with care and purpose. The top of his scalp was scored with four tight braids that fell in twists to his shoulders. The braids were wrapped with swirls of copper wire that ended in crooked-edged loops, each wrapping a clear, green stone.

Hinfūs growled again. I brushed my fingers at my side, and my hound stopped, backed into the shadows and gave a grunt as he lay down.

I took a step forward to look more closely at the stones. Immediately, the man turned his oval face, his uncanny green eyes piercing the distance between us. His lips were ringed with tattoos and above, the slits at the bottom of his flat-bridged nose blinked like side-ways eyes. I had once seen a nose like his on a warrior who had been burned in the face. That warrior had not unnerved me, for I knew what caused his disfigurement.

This man did not look made. He looked born. Born with cheek-bones that were flat and extra skin that hung down along his jaw like a flapping curtain. Each ear was punctured with a large piece of the twist-ed wood from the wall. The skin puckered angrily around the slivers. I wondered if this was how he controlled movement through the barrier.

I moved to him and pulled one of the wooden slivers from his ear. Blood pooled on his lobe, but he did not cry out. Instead, he sniffed loudly at the air as if to draw in my scent. I stepped away from his strangeness, twirling the wood in my fingers.

"Does this bind to your blood and allow you to pass through the wall?"

In the dimness of the tent, the tattoos made his mouth seem unnaturally large. The man jerked forward, but the ropes stopped his body before he could reach me. He grunted, the cords in his neck standing out against the coarse rope wrapped above his collar bone.

I ignored his futile struggles and glanced over his thin hairless chest and sagging stomach. The panting heaved his guts over the rectangle of soft animal hide that hung over his groin. The loincloth was marked with lightly burned symbols of half-moons and snaking lines.

When I did not move to harm him, or respond to his display of anger, the man stopped straining. The sweat of his fear filled the air with an oily, pungent scent.

His helpless struggling convinced me he was nothing more than a savage. I loosened the clasp of my cape and pulled the hood from my head. As I was revealed, the man's breath hissed through his teeth. His green eyes roved over my height, crawling up my torso to the top of my head.

Let him read my hair, wild with knots, to know the soul he dealt with.

"What tribe do you hail from?" I asked, holding my head high and looking down my nose at his smaller stature.

He pulled back his lips in a sneer and his bottom lip cracked.

I reached up and unhooked my water flask from a hook. I had not had my evening drink, and though it was not yet time, I sucked just enough to pool on my tongue. I held the water in my mouth, then swallowed the trickle.

The man's apple bobbed with thirst, but his gaze was steady.

I held the water flask up to him and raised my brows.

A click sounded as his throat tried to swallow what little spit he had left.

I moved slowly forward, keeping my eyes on his, and placed the spout of the flask against his bottom lip. He latched onto the bag, sucking like a calf at its mother's teat. I allowed him two swallows before I pulled away the skin, popping his thick lips with a loud smack. His eyes roved over me eagerly as he licked the drops from his tattooed mouth.

That's when I saw his tongue was pierced with a copper ring that glittered with a small tear-shaped, green stone, just like the stones in his hair. When he read the direction of my eyes, he pressed his lips together and quickly turned his head to the side.

I reached out and grabbed him by the jaw. Twisting the loose skin under my forceful grip, I pried his jaws open. Within his mouth, his tongue leapt from side to side, as if to escape me. The swinging gem knocked against his tooth, and a pure clear note found its way to my ear, ringing into silence. My wound-hound rose from its resting place by the pile of furs, whining for the source.

"Ring the rump," the flanks had said about the twisted wood.

I released the man and stepped back. His mouth tattoos merged with his newly bruised skin. I looked closer at the pattern of circles interlinking around his lips. He frowned at my study of his face and sucked his lips into his mouth until all the loose skin and his tattoos were pulled in between his teeth.

Hinfūs growled at this strangeness. I waved my hound back, though I too was disturbed.

The captive's spirit shone through his eyes, challenging me. I could see his inner strength, and though it thrilled me to imagine breaking him. But we did not have time for such games. Each day, we used more of our water and supplies. I needed to breach the wall and get into the District.

Torment aside, my other option was to use Lumen. There was always risk in opening a bridge to my mind with the medallion. I rubbed my teeth against each other as I weighed the idea. The captive did not break eye contact, and his raw challenge aided my decision.

I touched Lumen with my thoughts and felt it thrum to life. Then, I imagined a thought strike, and before a heartbeat had passed, the man arched on the pole. His eyes rolled, glaring white in his darker face. His lips popped from his mouth as it grew slack. The tension dropped from his body, and he slumped in the bindings, drool stringing off his slack lips. Those challenging eyes were now closed.

"Saigire," I commanded the disc

I created an image of the man on a journey, tracing events backwards from where we stood at this moment, to when I had first seen Rserker and his men enter the camp. Lumen prodded this into the captive's mind, which continued with the rest, feeding me his memory. I led the way by imagining the thorny wall as he had crossed through it with six from the inside.

The captive moaned, his eyelids fluttering but never opening.

I was surprised. Lumen cast no sensation when I did a seek, yet the captive seemed to know what I was up to. Never had I seen such defiance of Lumen's delving.

Even as I thought it, the captive was becoming more aware, his body taking up the battle. He strained against the tent pole, thrashing his head from side to side as if being beaten.

It did not matter; his struggling could not stop me. I ignored his half-conscious writhing, focusing instead on the answer I sought. Lumen dug deeper into his core. There were many strange thoughts and images within him I did not understand. I passed them quickly, blurring them behind my seek like fog stirring over water. Moving backward through his memory, a tune flipped up like a loose stone and tripped my search. I discovered his view of the Hæsel wood wall.

He threw back his head and howled like a beast. Hinfūs scrambled up from his resting place, growling and snapping at the captive's legs.

I ran Lumen over the memory again. There was a pause as the group waited on the inside of the barrier, then that note, a tune played. I had heard a note within, once before. It was of the same pitch made by the jewel in the captive's mouth, but this was a song, and there was a second player, a melody twisting around the first.

I ran the memory one last time, until I was sure I had the tune in my own mind. Then, I pulled out of the seek and looked into the man's open eyes. My lips curled in triumph.

"Do you wish to speak now?" I asked him.

His entire body trembled with rage. But he dropped his gaze, his lashes thick and lush against his flat cheeks. I stepped closer, basking in his defeat, when suddenly, his chin shot up and then he was there, in front of me, and I was caught by the intense green of his eyes. How strange it was that his pupils were no longer round but squeezed into oval slits.

Unnerved, I stepped back but spoke brave words. "I do not know what manner of man you are, but I know your secrets."

He howled again and thrashed against the ropes like a tormented beast.

"Slæpen," I whispered, and Lumen sent the man to darkness. I watched with relief as his lids closed over his unnatural eyes.

Pulling on my hood, I left the tent.

The flanks were half squatting on their hinds when I passed them. They rushed to follow me, but I sent them back to the tent's entrance to guard the captive. I wasn't sure how long the sleep would hold, and I did not want Hinfūs to chew the meat from his bones. Not until I had what I needed.

Night had grown late, while I had been using Lumen. Dying embers cooled in the shallow pits, and snores rose on the cooling air. Few were about to witness me slipping between the tents.

I slowed as I came upon Rserker and his group. His warriors squatted together, speaking in quiet voices. One threw out his arm in a game of throwing bones. The captives dozed among them. Rserker became aware of my presence and rose to greet me. Though he knew my nightsight was a blessing, he held his torch high to light the last few feet between us.

"All is well?"

"Hm," he grunted.

Stepping closer, he tipped his face closer to the opening of my hood.

"What did you learn from the man?" he whispered.

I pushed back the material. "He gave nothing willingly."

Moving away from my General, I approached the nearest bound woman. She was sleeping, curled in the dust like a wood rodent. I pushed her with my foot. She awoke, looked up at me standing in front of the flickering torch and gave a short whine. Quickly pulling her legs to one side under her, she sat up on one hip. I looked down into her frightened face with intent.

"Open." I pointed at her mouth.

Her head shivered.

Using my hands, I motioned for her to open her lips. She continued to shake, but stubbornly set her jaw.

Pulling my dagger from my thigh sheath, I dropped on to her body with my knees. She grunted and fell to the side, her bound hands useless. Grasping her chin with one hand, I pressed the cross guard of my dagger into the space behind her molars and pried. She released her jaw muscles with a whimper.

"Pull out her tongue," I demanded.

Rserker had stood watching me in silence, but now he moved. Kneeling beside me, he pressed the heat of his shoulder against mine and pushed his large fingers into the woman's mouth while I held her teeth apart. She shook her head, dislodging my dagger.

"Hound's death!" Rserker cursed and yanked back his hand. He put his finger into his mouth to suck at the bite she had given him.

Angry at the wasted time, I laid my full weight on her, pushing her head into the dirt with my forearm. With my other hand, I pried with the dagger until I was sure I had her mouth secured.

"Her tongue!" I barked at Rserker.

He leaned in, practically on my back as he reached into her bruised lips. His breath was hot in my ear as he struggled with her.

The captive gagged on his hand, and I felt her body heave up under mine.

"And a slippery one it is!" Rserker laughed, pulling the end into view.

I looked closely. It was not pierced.

"Leave her." I sheathed my dagger and stood.

Turning to the others, I saw they were all awake, watching in silence.

"The next!"

Rserker motioned for his guards to aid. Each stubborn, tattooed mouth was pried open, but none had a tongue jewel like the leader.

In the captive's memory, I *had* heard two tunes, and I was sure two notes were needed to straighten the wood. But where was the other one?

I looked around the group for the answer. The first woman's eyes slid a little to the side. I followed her gaze and saw the slumped shadow far from the edge of the campfire light.

"There." I pointed.

"Dead. I had her dragged away from the rest."

Rserker and I moved toward the still figure. As his torch's light led the way to her body, it rose on the mound of her stomach, hard and round. I faltered.

Rserker spoke quickly, "She bloats from the acids within her. Her stomach was flat when she fell."

Relief washed over my skull, leaving my hair prickling on my head. If we had killed a woman with child, after everything we had done to find one...

A chill ran down the outside of my arms, and I blinked to clear my thoughts. Rserker jabbed the torch's handle into the dirt and knelt by the woman. His beard cast a shadow on the death-wound. It gaped in her breast, the fat pressing out of a slit above her dark, round nipple. In death, the woman's neck could no longer support her head and it lay awkwardly on her shoulder. She looked much like the man in my tent, but her face was tattoo-free.

I knelt to the task and turned her face to me. Her mouth was slack, easy to open. Rserker moved the torch closer. A sparkle winked in the black hole within her face. The jewel was there.

I lifted her soft tongue, but as I pulled, a liquid squirted out from underneath and struck my face with a wet slap. I fell back against Rserker's knees, smearing the mucus across my skin. Rolling, I spit in the dust trying to free my mouth of the bitter tasting paste.

"Laywren!" Rserker stood over me, ready with his water flask.

As if from far away, I could hear the captives chanting in low voices.

I got up on my knees and tilted my face up to him, opening my lids for the washing. The warm water showered over my skin and into my eyes and mouth. This time it was I who latched onto the water flask like a calf, sucking until I could fill my mouth with the liquid. I rinsed the water around my teeth and spat it to the ground. Rserker knelt before me and used the corner of his cloak to wipe my face. His brow was creased with concern.

"Do you feel ill?" He asked as he ran the cloth over my lips, cleansing them.

I slipped inside, sending Lumen scurrying through my body. My blood flowed with even rhythm, my thoughts were sharp, my stomach's acid did not rise or revolt. I looked at Rserker's face, and it did not blur.

"I am well," I answered.

Rserker stood and reached down a hand to pull me up.

I ignored it and stood. "I am better than she."

He snorted, then picked up the torch. This time, we approached the woman with more caution. I walked around her twice, listening to the others chanting in words I could not understand. The guards spoke roughly to them, but they did not stop.

Convinced nothing else would shoot out of her dead body, I knelt by her engorged stomach. The eerie thought of an unborn kicking against my palm crept into my mind. The skin was stretched tight across her bloat, widening what had probably been a smaller tattoo. Around her birth knot were three joining rings.

"Look here," I said to Rserker as I dragged a finger across the symbols on her skin.

"The sign of the balance," Rserker observed.

"It is not balanced. Look closer."

He leaned over her stomach, holding the torch just above her brown skin. One ring was missing, and in its place, a snake was swallowing its own tail. I ran my hand across her distended belly to her hip bone where a creature was drawn upon her in blue. The square muzzle on the creature marked it as a wound-hound. The hound was running, its legs splayed out as it leapt across her skin, a ring clutched in its fanged jaws.

"What do you think is the meaning?" I asked Rserker.

"I know not, Laywren." He ran his hand down his beard. "Perhaps, Dorn is needed."

I gave a small nod.

We needed to get past the twisted Hæsel and into the District, first. Then, I would consider these markings.

I moved back to the woman's mouth. Keeping my head to the side, I cautiously lifted her tongue to reveal the empty sack beneath.

"Careful." Rserker's teeth flashed in the night, as he brought the torch closer.

I shook her tongue to flick the jewel against a tooth. A note echoed within her mouth, lifting to my ears softly. Rserker's expression did not change. I realized he could not hear it, but he had seen what I did.

"Shall I cut her tongue out?" he asked.

I released her tongue and nodded, dropping the jewel against another tooth. This time the note was different, thick and sweet like the Hum-fly's song.

"Hold." I placed my hand upon his.

Again, I lifted her tongue within the circle of her teeth and this time, I struck the jewel against a different tooth. This note rippled deep in my sinuses, unlike the first two sounds. I cursed at my near mistake. Taking out my dagger, I slit the end of her tongue, retrieving the ring.

"I need her teeth in place," I said to Rserker before rising and walking back past the captives.

They had stopped their chant. I could feel the heat of hatred in their gazes as I passed them. The sound of Rserker's sword cleaving the woman's neck took their minds off me.

Away from the group, I paused in the light of the moon to look closely at the little green jewel. Spitting on it, I rubbed it between my rough-skinned fingers. Its cut edges caught the silver moonlight and reflected the colour of the male captive's eyes. I tucked the jewel into my pouch with the goddess statue.

The captive's people were strange, unlike any I had met. I had many questions about the markings on the dead woman's skin. I was sure her tattoos were not just for decoration, for they held the rings of the cycle, and therefore must hold a meaning for us. I tapped into Lumen and sent a message to Rserker.

~ Do not allow the Griffain to take the dead woman ~

For now, I would return to the captive in my tent to see if I could extract more knowledge. For that, I needed to be alone.

I would have Dorn examine the woman's tattoos in the morning. I also desired his thoughts on why these strangers had been in the District. They were clearly a different tribe from those who had battled us from behind the wall. Mixed tribes were rare in settlements, for strength was found in sameness.

My people were mixed, only because we took on others through the borh-hand when our numbers fell to the battles. Though we were of different tribes, the Horde was *one*. Not because of our skin or our language, but because we worshipped the one true goddess and lived to serve her.

I looked up at the moon that coursed its way to dawn and spoke a prayer of thanks to Goddess for I was sure I would find the way to breach the wall, now that I had the jewel.

Chapter 6: Skulls and Scales and Hoarge Mount Tales

It was still dark when I re-entered my tent. The flanks followed behind me, ready to bed down for what was left of the night. The captive lifted his head and his eyes tracked my movements. Lumen's sleep had done him good, for he seemed more alert.

The flanks snuffled and scuffed the tent as they settled in their corner. Hinfūs stirred and grunted, sniffing the air. I lifted the skin and he bounded off into the dark to hunt. On my way to the back of the tent, I stopped to test the tautness of the captive's bindings. He sniffed the air behind me as I passed him. I wondered if he could smell his woman's spit on my skin, or perhaps her death.

When I was sure he was secure, I made my way to my sleeping furs, which were mounded on the tent floor. I thought of the woman's bloated stomach. It was a vessel, but not for a child. Would that it had been a child, for to know it was still possible...

A deep tiredness washed over me, thinning out any desire I had to question the captive. I drew in a long breath, expanding my chest until my armour became tight. I held it until my lungs ached.

Sometimes, as life became more desperate and my actions became crueller, I feared the goddess' light was leaving me. Then I would imagine darkness was pulling me down.

The captive pushed at the ground with his cracked heels, attempting to spin himself around the pole to better see me. I could not use Lumen when I was weakened. It was too dangerous. And, I was weakened—weakened by waiting, weakened by holding to my beliefs in something that was fast fading.

Tomorrow, I would find a way to make the captive talk. Tomorrow, I would be stronger.

Sitting on the floor, I unlaced my leather shin and forearm guards. Leaving my woolen shirt on, I settled down with my daggers within reach of my hands.

Before falling asleep, I looked at the captive's back where he was tied against the stake. He had stopped squirming and his hands were resting on the pole, palms out, his wrists red and swollen beneath the cord. Lying down, I closed my heavy lids as the air lifted the last drops of sweat from my body. Through my lashes, I saw the man's fingers shaping themselves into signs.

Quickly, I opened my eyes and rose on my elbow to observe the strange motioning, but his hands had stopped. I could hear the rough snoring of the flanks as they slept. I did not take my eyes from the man. He was cast pale in the blue light of the moon that shone straight down through the tent's air hole. The moon's light set the green stones in his hair glowing like fairy wings. A chill against my neck warned me to be cautious.

I rose and carefully moved around him. His head was down, and I could not tell if he was asleep or awake. As I stopped before him, a quick twist of his neck brought his head up and he locked onto my face with his strange eyes. A brilliant green glow started up in the midpoint of his orbs and spread to the edges of his lashes.

I was taken by the light.

Without my command, Lumen tugged at my mind like a fish on a line.

The man opened his mouth wide releasing the jewel's shimmer from the cavern in his face. He flicked his thin red tongue against his teeth creating a sweet and longing tune of five notes. Lumen showed me an image of the wood unfurling from around the District.

"I offers you this key," he hissed.

I leaned closer to see which teeth the man tapped the green crystal against. But his tongue slid out towards me, the jewel twinkling in the moon light.

Understanding, I opened my mouth to accept his offer. As our faces met, his lips pressed against mine, soft and yielding. I felt the jewel knock against my teeth, the pitch rising and falling with each tap as he tuned my mouth. The notes journeyed deep into my skull, and my mind turned inward following the echo's path.

~ I would hold you ~ his voice whispered in my thoughts.

The last ringing note was muffled as his tongue swelled in my mouth. The thickness grew, forcing my jaws to open until my joints crackled like popping tendons. I wanted to push him away, but my arms stayed lax at my sides. I could not command them.

Inside the soft tissues of my mouth, his tongue lengthened, forcing its way down my throat. I gagged, twice, heaving on his flesh before I could control my reflex. I tried to stay calm, to breathe slowly, my nostrils sucking in what air they could. The slithering length worked its way deeper into my body, and I imagined the jewel glowing within my guts. I tried to pace my breath, maintaining a rhythm that would feed my life, but alarm was increasing my heart rate.

I strained to send a siren to the flanks through Lumen, but there was no response. It was no longer in my control. My disc had become the binding bridge between the captive and my will. Making sound was impossible, and my eyes were blinded by the man's face tight against mine.

Blackness pushed in at the edges of my sight. Slow and steady, I calmed my heart, slackening my breathing until it no longer whistled through my nostrils.

Suddenly, a seeking brushed my thigh. Something cold and smooth wriggled between my legs, pressing to enter. It felt more like a burrowing animal than a man's urgency. I tried to squeeze my thighs together, but like my arms, my lower limbs were dead to my command.

The thick length glided into my flesh, winding up through the warm cradle of my womb. The two ends of the man moved within my body, piercing me as the copper ring pierced his tongue. And, as I drowned for air, I saw a vision.

Rows of green and black shields rose in the darkness. Four shields were flipped back and behind each was a skin pouch. In each pouch was a green gem—radiant within its crib. Within the gems, tiny peach-coloured, bean-shaped creatures turned, floating in the light.

Intrigued, I watched the roll of one frail, curled body. The bones of its spine pressed out against its translucent skin reminding me of the dried carcasses spread throughout the desert. The tiny thing floated slowly around until it faced me with overlarge, black eyes, blank above a bulbous brow. Below its inverted nose, a mouth, an empty gape, opened and through it floated a cry that turned my blood to stone.

"Módor," it wailed.

MY HANDS CLAWED THICK fur as I startled the rest of the way into wakefulness. My eyes burned with grit. I rapidly blinked to bring the inside of my tent into focus.

All was silent and still in the early dawn light, but not in my memory.

Rising quickly to my feet, I pulled my sword from its scabbard before the film of sleep could be fully blinked away. Attuned to my alarm, the flanks rose on their crooked legs, their bodies bent in a defensive posture as they sought to find the threat.

In the midpoint of the tent, the captive hung from the stake, just as he had when I had fallen asleep. I mind-touched Lumen and found it open to my control.

Narrowing my eyes, I cautiously moved towards the man, circling wide around the stake until I faced him once again. His chin hung down at a strange angle, hiding the rope that wrapped his neck. The cord on his chest held his body upright, but his legs were lax, unnaturally so. The way the man's body drooped made the hair on my arms crawl like beetles.

"Wake!" I commanded him, jabbing my sword at the air before his heart.

The flanks moved in close behind me, their claws extended.

I jabbed at his chest, a second time. "Wake and speak, Wyccum!"

The point of my sword slid without resistance into the man's chest cavity, but it broke no skin. It just pushed his skin in. Dread pebbled the surface of my skull. I lowered my sword and reached out. The grey of my skin looked dead next to his faded copper tones. I pushed my hand into his torso. His skin yielded like an unfilled sack.

Aghast, I stepped back and whispered, "He is empty."

The flanks clicked in their bug-like language. Lumen translated.

Left Flank ~ He is gone ~

I followed the flank's gaze to the tent's air hole. A delicate white fabric was clinging where the poles met. Reaching up with the end of my sword, I gently lifted it down. It was almost transparent, flat and thin, as long as my leg and twice as wide. Jagged along the edges, it looked as if it had been torn from its source.

A scale pattern had been pressed into its paper surface, and that's what told me it was skin—shed skin. Holding it closer in the dim light, I measured the scale size—each was as wide as my palm.

Frowning, I looked at the man's husk slumped against the pole and back to the tent's air hole, which was not wide enough for a man to pass.

"Check outside."

The Flanks moved out and I quickly donned my armour and strapped my arrow quiver to my back. My bow would serve me at a distance, my daggers in close combat. I wasn't sure what I was hunting, but I would be prepared.

ON THE OUTSKIRTS OF the camp, Rserker was kneeling and running his hand along the ground. As I approached, I counted the heads of the captives. All were present.

"Here," Rserker wasted no time in greeting, only showed me a track in the dust when I was alongside him.

The track was three feet wide and rippled like a wave into the wood.

"One of the pacers saw it move into the forest. She says it was long and thin..." He paused and looked at me with doubt. "...like a serpent."

I nodded. The pieces fit together in my mind. "It is the male captive."

Rserker frowned. "It took the dead woman."

We backtracked its path to where she had lain. The soil was stained with blood from the removal of her skull. I was dissatisfied Dorn would not get a chance to examine the captive woman's tattoos.

"Her teeth?" I asked, frustration building inside of me.

"Ours."

I wanted to hunt the serpent myself, but I had to speak to Dorn. I needed his wisdom.

"Have your men track it down and bring back its head." I broiled with simmering anger as I remembered the captive's touch. "And, I would have its skin."

"What about the others?" Rserker motioned to the captives.

"Sack and hang them."

I did not know what shape these people could take, but the sacks of tightly woven grasses could hold all but the finest grains of sand.

"Where are the woman's teeth?"

"Cook is boiling her skull down," Rserker said. "Don't eat the mid-day broth," he added as an afterthought.

His last words were spoken to my back as I left for the cook's area.

THE SUN HAD JUST BEGUN to peek over the horizon when I entered the bustling of the cooking area that usually started before first light. A pot of blackened iron hung from a three-stick support. Within the pot, gruel was bubbling thickly around a wooden spoon sticking past the lip.

The three, balding cooks stood by the fire, singing a song to the morning meal. Their puffy, white flesh and shedding black hair gave them a diseased look, but they were vigorous enough to be testy to those who interrupted their ritual morning chant. I slowed my approach to let them finish.

The apple bobs
a boney cob.
And shreds its skin
to show its grin.
A toothy tune,
a boney rune.
A song to make
the curl wood straight!

The three chanted together and I was struck, as always, by their oddness. Their tribe and their name were unknown. All responded to "cook."

One turned my way, and then, quickly scuffled to a smaller pot boiling steamy bubbles past its lid. I followed.

With long tongs, Cook gently lifted out the woman's skull. A few pieces of flesh clung stubbornly to the bone, but Cook shook it in the liquid, dislodging these last memories of life. Placing the skull in a wooden bowl, the hag passed it to me. White swirls of steam rose out of the black eye sockets. I imagined it was the dead woman's soul rising to the Hall and took care not to breathe it in.

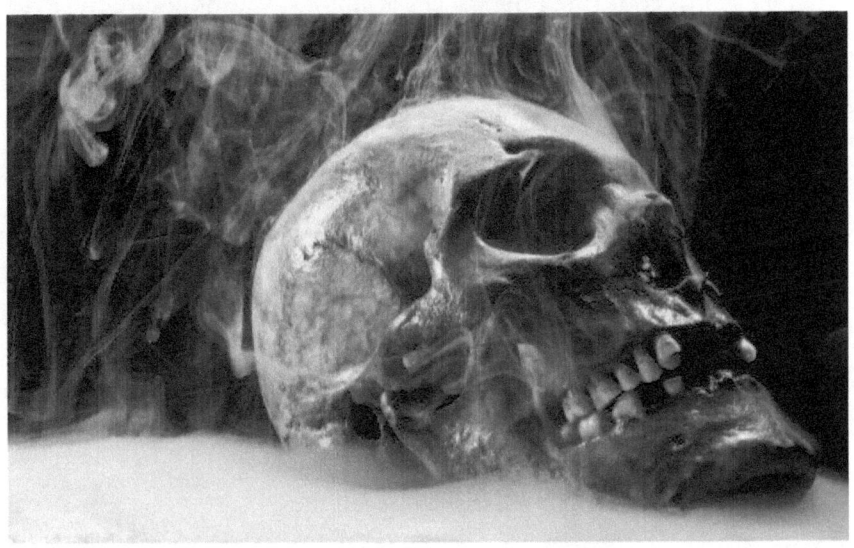

COOK LEANED CLOSE TO me, breathing the odor of burnt garlic out through short stubs of rotten teeth.

"Beware the notes, for they would float you into a mist of mindly list." She reached under her arm to scratch madly at her moss-like armpit hair.

I looked intensely at the woman. She was soft on the outside, but the inside was full of stealth. "What do you know of these notes?"

She cackled and did a little dance. "The sound is the mount, and the mount is the quest, and the treasure bequeath, that which you want best," she sang.

Her words fell upon my mind like stones on dirt.

I handed her the piece of white skin that had been left hanging in my tent. "Tell me straight," I ordered. "What sheds this?"

Cook stepped forward and clutched it from my hands. She sniffed it, licked it and looked at the rising sun through it.

"It is as it shed," she said.

"No riddles," I warned, holding up my finger.

"A snake! A snake!" she shrieked, running off with the skin.

Her words confirmed the pacer's account. I was now sure the male captive had somehow changed into a serpent. It takes powerful magicks to shift from one form to another. Or perhaps the captive was a serpent who had worn a fleshy disguise. It mattered little, for Rserker's warriors would soon return with word that it was slain, and what it was, it would no longer be.

I gave the still-warm skull my attention. The song Lumen had taken from the captive's memories was the tune to exit from the District. But the song he had given me in my vision, was the tune to enter. A thrill slicked my guts as the notes danced in my memory. It was time to open the wall of thorns.

"Spill the pot," I yelled to Cook as I turned to go.

I did not look back to see if she obeyed me.

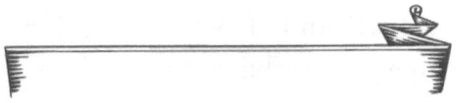

Chapter 7: Planning the Attack

Dorn, Rserker and I were speaking loudly as we planned our strategy. Our hearts glowed heartily, for it was possible we could finally breach the wall of our enemy.

I had also invited Nethaz to attend the war talk. The giant sat cross-legged on the floor, filling my tent with his bulk. I wanted to be assured of his loyalty and draw upon whatever battle-planning skills he might have.

Dorn had stood close to my side as we planned, but now the heat of his body took my mind from my task. I stepped away, putting some distance between us and looked to Rserker, who stood behind Nethaz.

"We attack at dawn." I said. "I would taste bread by midday."

Dorn and Rserker nodded, grins silly upon their faces as they thought of the water, food and even possibly of children who could be in the District.

Nethaz stayed solemn and turned his sky-blue eyes my way. "We've beaten their best on the battlefield," he rumbled in his low voice. "Can we not ask for bread?"

Silence cut the air.

Rserker slapped his hand onto Nethaz's shoulder. "Ask them for their untouched women, too," he laughed, trying to make light of the giant's question.

Dorn, who sometimes could not contain his advice, intoned, "The great warrior, Gonzoeh, would dip his sword into wanton feasts, and wanting more, he fired his blade, in the heart of a burning wreath."

Rserker frowned at Dorn and took his hand from the giant's shoulder. "Release me from your teachings, Warden."

Dorn looked down to hide a smile.

I did not let the prattle of Dorn and Rserker distract me from Nethaz's request. His eyes were locked onto mine, waiting for my answer.

"They will kill you before you speak," I warned.

"I will not approach them as a warrior."

"The warrior who lays down his-" Dorn began.

I cut him off. "What will you approach them as?"

"Ask them for their jewels, and I will present them to our Queen," Rserker bowed deeply to me.

I waved him away, keeping my eyes on the giant.

"A trader," Nethaz slowly stood. His head pressed up against the tent roof, and we all took a step back.

The giant still looked to me for permission. "I would approach them as a trader," he repeated.

"You have nothing to trade," I reminded him, wondering what he might think he could barter.

Rserker had stilled, and Dorn was finally, carefully silent.

"If you announce yourself, you will alert their guard that we are done with waiting." I slowly pulled my sword from its sheath and pointed it at the giant's guts to add weight to my words. "And that would be considered a betrayal of the Horde."

Nethaz spread his hands, "That would not be my intention."

"But it would be the result, which is just as damning."

Dorn waited, his eyes darting between us. Rserker's hand moved to rest lightly on the pommel of his sword. The giant's insolence was unbearable. I wanted to strike him down for the likelihood that he would become a traitor but could clearly see there was no anger in Nethaz, no disrespect even though his words should never have been spoken. He stood looking down on me with his face full of hope.

I held Nethaz's gaze until I was sure he understood how dangerously close he was treading.

Finally, he lowered his eyes and spoke. "What is your command, my Queen?"

I remembered what the giant had said about the trapped souls in the Hall. I knew he felt that our warring would only worsen our lot. I met Rserker's eyes knowing he was waiting for my order. Cutting the giant down would lose a mighty warrior I had need of. Letting him live left me crawling with doubt, alert to the threat of his strange ideas and ways.

I lowered my eyes from my general's silent question and sheathed my sword. "See if you can rouse an army from those who have grown lazy in waiting. We will enter the East wall at dawn," I ordered.

Rserker gave a curt nod. His face was full of shame for Nethaz was his wúsc-bearn. "I will instruct him better, Sister," he promised before bowing.

Rserker left, motioning for the giant to follow. Nethaz squeezed out of the tent's slit, the hides stretching over his broad shoulders.

From outside, came the sound of a solid slap followed by Rserker's angry words. "You can thank the goddess for your life!" he barked.

Dorn's warm voice drew my attention back inside the tent. "A wise leader weighs the scales, and listens to the warden's tales, and from the mind, and to the mouth, wisdom flows like silver trout."

"Ha!" I scorned. "Bread will flow to my mouth delivered on a river of blood, and I shall be Queen, evermore."

These were brave words, and I held my stance a moment beyond them. Then, I smiled and moved to sit down and listen to my mentor's words. He was clearly bursting to advise me.

"Once, only once, never twice and not thrice, a Queen was born with a blessing from the goddess." Dorn sat down in front of me, pulling his sandaled feet in under his strong calves.

His knee was touching mine, and I shifted backwards. Then, I rested my hands in my lap and smiled at Dorn, ready for his words.

Dorn studied my face before speaking. I wondered what he was thinking, what he was plotting. He reached out his right hand, holding it in the air between us, waiting. I frowned at his hand and looked up to see his eyes twinkling at my discomfort. My face reddened under his glance, but I did not give him my hand. He shrugged good-naturedly and placed his hand on his knee before he continued his story.

"And, all who saw her, all who heard her speak and watched her lead, and all who felt her strength of spirit, followed the Queen," he recited in his storyteller's rhythm. "And the Horde grew. And, the weight of the problems pressed. Yet, the leader's shoulders never bowed, for she was chosen to be challenged, born to abide the sorrows of her time, set apart to walk alone..."

Again, Dorn reached out his hand. I looked at his palm hanging in the air between us and then back at his face. His playfulness was gone.

Sighing dramatically, I placed my hand in his as if we would shake.

"What is it that you are up to Warden?" I asked.

But Dorn only smiled encouragingly and squeezed my hand. His skin was warm, the calluses scratching my palm with little thrills.

"And all who followed the Queen, pledged their lives to Goddess, through her." He turned over my sword hand and looked at the skin of my palm.

I enjoyed his touch, but I was guarded. Dorn usually stood to tell a tale, pacing back and forth, acting out the words. Never had he sat before me so closely. Never had he focused on me so intently.

His eyes rested on my mouth while he continued. "All swore loyalty to the Queen—to the DreÓdreng—warrior for Goddess. Some gave their lives and some..." Dorn lifted my hand to his lips and planted a kiss on the top of my knuckles. "...gave their love."

My lips parted. He was serious, as serious as any man pledging to the woman of his choice. I yanked my hand from his.

"I thought you were going to tell me a tale!" I accused, standing in one fluid movement.

Dorn slowly stood and bowed as if my obedient servant, yet I felt he was in control of both of us. "Tales come in twos. The story happens, and the telling follows. Which do you need first?"

My insides bristled at his choice of words. I turned my gaze to ice. "What I need, Chronicle Warden, is time alone to plan tomorrow's attack."

Dorn's amber eyes sparked at my tone. We stood face-to-face, and I could hear my own breathing.

"Alone."

A muscle jumped in Dorn's jaw, and for a moment, I did not know what he would dare. My eyes narrowed in warning. Then, Dorn lowered his gaze to the ground. His face softened as he calmed. When he raised his head, his lips were set with resolve. He bowed and left my tent.

I placed my hand against my throat. My pulse leapt like a trapped rabbit. Dorn had never asked for more than to serve me, and I had been glad of that. I had been content to avoid anything that could affect my rule.

And yet, I was not overly displeased that he had taken this next step. In fact, if he had chosen a different night, a different approach, I may have been able to accept him.

A tightness in my chest rose at the thought.

Dorn was the man I respected enough to be with, but allowing my feelings for him to grow would put me in a vulnerable state. I could not afford to need any man. I could not meet the expense of need and still control the Horde.

WHEN I HAD BEEN A CHILD, I had been consumed by a desire to please my father with the right answers to his questions. But more so,

I was determined to get my own way, and one day, that added scheme had led to a battle of wills between my sire and me.

"The marauder wants; the quarry needs," my father had said. "Which do you want to be?"

I had leapt from his lap, bracing my feet on the stones in front of our home and waving my arm as if it held a dagger.

"I want to be a marauder!" I had shouted.

My father had looked sternly at me from beneath grey, furry brows. His hair wild around his jagged features—clouds of grey, brownish wisps flying free from a braid that could never contain his magnificent mane.

"To want is to wish," he said in his Overland lilt. "If you only wish for it, you can plan to seize it, for your mind will be clear from the craze of your heart."

"But to need!" Father slammed his hand on his knee, making an old scar stand out white on the reddened flesh. "To need is to cloud your mind. To need is to weaken your will. To need is to be unable to walk away when you cannot take hold of what you must have."

I shuffled my feet, feeling a child's guilt for my earlier claim that I needed a new mount.

"To need that which you cannot grasp," Father lifted his thick fist and pointed a finger at me. "That is when you are open to danger."

I looked up past his metal-studded, leather armour, past his grizzled beard, to find those hard, grey eyes glinting down at me. He towered, so far above, it seemed as if his head was in the clouds. I knew he wanted me to understand I should never, ever need anything, but I had driven my hoarge to death riding over the shale hills, and I needed another.

"Very well, father." I pushed my chin out even further and put my hands on my slim hips. "I *want* another hoarge mount," I finished with a little nod.

"Hmmmmmm," the growl came deep from my father's chest as he looked down on me with stormy disapproval. My skinny arms fell to my sides in defeat.

"You will keep at drill on foot." He placed his large hand on top of my head. "This is the price you pay for killing a good mount."

My heart pounded in my young chest, pumping blood into arms and legs that wanted to fling themselves out in fury. But I dared not. My father's wrath was many times more frightening than mine.

My breath came loud and jagged as I gave him the expected response. "Yes, father." My lips pressed tight after the words.

He grabbed me by the chin and knelt to look into my eyes, which were tearing up with unreleased anger. Roughly, he smeared a tear across my cheek with his thumb.

"This is need. Learn to run the shale on foot, and you will no longer need a mount."

And, he was right. I had continued my training on the shale hills. The first few days taught me that to fall was to be shredded on the sharp stone edges. So, I had wrapped my legs in leather straps to mid-thigh. I had wrapped my hands and my elbows. Each day, I spilled less blood and in months became almost as agile as the hoarge mount with its folding, calloused feet. I did not ask for another mount for almost eight months. And when I did, it was because I wanted it, not because I needed it.

Chapter 8: Poison on the Thorns

E ach step we took on the undefended, grassless field pounded out the warning of our approach. We were thirty-two strong, and we were armed. There were no bodies to step over for the dead had been carried to the skies in the clutches of the Griffain. There were none left living that could resist our coming. Ahead of us the blinding-white wall of twisted wood barred our way, bristling with thorns.

At the east side of the District, I motioned the warriors to a halt. Rserker's men relayed the order to those who were behind me. Their shouts took flight like startled birds on the morning air. The sentinel pacer walked with me to the wall to show the spot where she had seen the seven come through. I released her to the forest, where she could watch from safety.

Rserker moved to stand at my left and tilted his head back to look at the barrier of sun-bleached branches. I got a rare glimpse under his beard where the skin on his neck was tight with anticipation.

The white skull felt light in my hands. I had practiced playing the jewel against the teeth for hours the night before. I had not slept until I could recreate the song the male captive had given me with his tongue.

I felt sure the notes would work. With my focus on getting into the District and raiding for supplies, I would not be tracking the captive. It was a clever move. He sacrificed all who were left behind the wall to ensure his escape. But it would only delay my hunt. The serpent underestimated my taste for vengeance. He had violated me. He would pay.

But for now, here and now, at the gates that had foiled us for too long, I would discover whether I was correct or whether two songs were needed to enter. With steady hands, I played to the wood, tapping the green jewel against the skull's lipless teeth.

The last clear note had not died out completely before the groaning began. I stepped away from the branches as they straightened like slender arms reaching out for us. A rushing sound of a storm in a forest assaulted our ears as a passage opened to the District.

I heard a cry of despair from within, but it was quickly drowned out by the victorious cheer of my warriors. I dropped the woman's skull and pulled my sword. The booted feet of those running behind my charge drove the bone into the dust.

Bellowing, we burst into the inner court of the District. I quickly scanned the area. It was empty of people. Only an old man stood between us and the reddish brown, mud huts. His back was bowed with age, and his muscles were tight like sun-dried meat. I slowed my run, until I was five feet from him. The rest of the Horde split and ran down the two sides of the District, swerving around the pottery and cooking wood littering the area. The old man tried to straighten to meet me. His breath pushed his ribs out before he spoke.

"YOU HAVE BESTED US in warfare. Now we challenge you to best us in honour. We ask that you take what you need and leave enough for us to live." His spittle bubbled white at the corners of his mouth.

I could understand his language without translation from Lumen, and I recognized his speech as one of surrender with condition. I was slightly amused, for this old man had no right to conditions. No warrior stood with him. It was clear that his warriors had all charged us outside the gates in their last battle, and that he and his people were conquered.

He glowered at me under balding brow ridges. I looked over the battle scars on his chest and thighs and saw that his bony hands held his staff with confidence. He was an aged warrior who had never had the honour of being killed in battle. Even now, he was giving up his right to die in fight, in order to barter for his people. I was able to be generous.

"Before we speak of conditions, tell me who will be found within these walls?"

The old man did not look away or bow his head. A shadow crossed his eyes, but it was not a lie. It was pain.

"You will not find babes," he said bitterly.

My disappointment rose like bile in my throat, but I shook it off. Children could be hidden well, and an honorable warrior would never reveal the hiding place.

"Grandfather," I bowed. "We ask only for that which we need. Those we take will be wúsc-bearn, and in time, will become members of the Horde."

His shock of white hair dipped forward as relief released the tension in his neck. Then, he seemed to not know what to do. He looked left and right, listening to my men and women shout to each other, as they gathered food, cider and bread. A few shocked cries rang out, but they would only be cries of capture. We had finished killing when the last District warrior fell in the battle, days before.

Dorn came up to me, smiling his pleasure at our victory.

"There is a well in the midpoint of the huts," he said.

"Have you tested it?" I asked.

"Not yet," he looked at the old man leaning on his staff. "But I will, and then we will draw the water off."

Admiration shone in his face. Breaching the District had been one more problem to overcome, and once done, I moved on. But Dorn liked to savour these triumphs, to raise them up higher than they were.

He would be weaving his tale of the jewel tune in his mind, and in a few nights, he would sing his praise of my skills. I was always uncomfortable with the attention Dorn directed my way as he turned me into a legend with his words. But at the same time, I was pleased for his stories strengthened the Horde's pledge. I did little for Dorn in return. I only led, but that seemed to be enough to keep him by my side.

Dorn walked toward the chaos of looting, untying his bag of herbs that he would use to test the water. He looked back over his shoulder and caught me watching him.

I quickly looked to the old warrior, who was tired of standing and had started lowering himself to the ground by sliding his hands down the staff. I realized this old one's mind would be full of tales of battles and stories of these lands. Stories that Dorn needed to make sense of the place. Grandfather would make a good gift—one that would show Dorn how I valued him. I moved forward and offered my arm to the old warrior.

"Come," I said. "Come and see the Horde."

He hesitated, looking behind him at the mud huts. Then he straightened and leaned heavily on the stick.

"You have spent many years behinds these walls, old man." I understood his regret in leaving and acknowledged his loss.

"Yes," he nodded, "I have been here many years, but the walls are new."

"Did it grow quickly?" I asked, curious about the wood, and the answers he might have.

He cleared his throat, loudly. "It was planted, by the others".

Before I could ask more, the old man shook his staff angrily at the sky. "One of many seeds that should never have been planted!" he shouted.

I watched the sagging skin of his arm flap with his movements and wondered at his words. "Were you captives of the dark-skinned ones?"

"Can one be willing and still be captive?" he asked.

"Hmmm," I grew tired of his riddles. I would give the old man to Dorn and let him find the answers.

"Come, old one." I led him toward the Horde. "There are three beauties who would stuff your sagging belly with stew." I was amused at the idea of the cooks being fine-looking.

We walked away from the sounds of pillaging and the District. I did not need to search the huts. Rserker knew what I wanted, what we all wanted. He and his men would be searching for children. For now, I had found my prize, and he stumbled on my arm with the weight of a feather. Half-way back to camp, I stopped, allowing him to catch his breath.

The old man turned his eyes to me. "I watched you battle in the field," he wheezed.

I looked up at the yellow sun. A Sicle bird screeched as it dove down onto an unwary lizard. I watched it rise on the wind, its prey writhing in its talons.

"You swing your long sword like an Overlander," he said when he had his breath.

I looked down into his eyes, half buried in wrinkled lids. "What do you know of the Overlanders?" I asked him.

"They were great wanderers. Some made it far into these lands." He puffed a bit, then said, "I must rest."

Sitting down on the ground, he barely got his legs crossed. But once settled, he reached to the side and ripped up a few blades of the parched grass that had been trampled in the battle. I watched him begin to weave a bridle rope pattern with the reeds.

Grandfather continued talking, his eyes on the daggers in my thigh sheaths. "You also carry the short swords of the Mantie Clan, though you lack the long arms to use them well."

I squatted in front of him, placing my elbows on my knees. "You know much of many."

He continued weaving, and I was impressed with the speed and surety of his knobby hands. When he did not speak again, I drew his question out.

"What is it you wish to ask, Grandfather?"

His hands stilled with the braided grass cradled gently between them. He lifted his head, taking a good long look at my face. "Most warriors fight in the way of their sires," he said.

I knew what he was looking for—the third eyelid of the Mantie. I stared back at him, unconcerned at his searching glance. I had long ago learned to control the instinct to film my eye under the heat and brightness of the sun.

MY MOTHER'S CLEAR, third eyelids slid in from the side, swiping sand from her eyes. The Overlanders were always unnerved by her, and I had vowed to never let my own lids slide across my gaze while they were looking.

The day I made that vow was burned into my memory. My mother had been drilling me in the way of the Mantie warrior. We stood facing each other while she adjusted my arms as if I were a puppet.

"Pull back your elbow."

"Turn the wrist, like so."

"Feet closer! On your toes!"

When she was sure my stance was perfect, we would begin the dance of the Mantie. Mountain peak! Snake strike! Eagle wing block! Hours and hours of her slashing at me and me trying to avoid her longer reach.

Once, some Overland children saw us and shouted jeers meant to sting my heritage. After that, my mother always made sure we practised closer to the village, where an audience could form. She felt the distraction of their taunts was good training for me, but I think she enjoyed showing off her speed and striking distance. She was deadly with the short dagger swords. But she was deadlier with her insight, always striking my rawest wounds with her words.

"You are Mantie and Overlander. You have a right to both, and will be accepted by neither," she would remind me as she adjusted my arms before we played for my father's kin.

I had tried not to look at the other children with their wide ribs and flat feet. I was tall and sleek like my mother, but I did not have the overlong Mantie arms needed to beat her in battle. On those days, under the children's mocking, I was glad to look a little less like her.

"LAYWREN!" DORN'S VOICE called me back from the past.

I turned and watched him run across the field toward us. His strong legs covered the distance much faster than we had. The old man continued weaving the grass, not looking up.

"The well is poisoned," Dorn's chest heaved with the effort of running in the day's heat. He leaned over, placing his hands on his knees and looked at the old man, while he panted for air. "There is no water for us, here," he said when he could speak.

"No water..." I repeated.

Looking away from Dorn, I released a slow, shaky breath. The waves of heat rippled in the air. We had stayed by the District, thinking that each day was one day closer to breaching the wall and getting supplies. Now those days were wasted, days we could have been traveling to a new water source. I sucked in a deep breath, tasting the air that held the threat of death.

"Grandfather," I waited until the old man twisted his neck to look up at me. "Did you poison the water?"

The old man looked down at his weaving hands. "Those who planted the wall did it before they left," he spoke bitterly.

I was relieved. I would not have to kill this proven warrior. But I was also surprised at the old man's claim of surrender with condition. Had we not come, those few left in the District would have eventually died of thirst.

I put my arm around Dorn's shoulder and moved him away from the old man, "Have you made sure no one will drink from the well?"

"Nethaz has placed a boulder over the top. None other than a giant can move it," he answered.

I had put off asking about the most precious bounty, because I feared the answer. But my desire to know something of worth was in the District, some justification for the time spent breaching the wall, urged me now to ask.

"Has Rserker found any children?"

Dorn's eyes dulled as he shook his head. "Not yet," he replied.

That loss of hope was like an arrow in my side.

"We need to clean out the District and move on," I said to Dorn.

Dorn shook his head. "There is time to celebrate this victory, Laywren."

"How are we victorious?" I sneered at the word.

Dorn took my shoulders and looked into my face with such faith, I had to look away. "Laywren, everything you do, every action you take, every decision you make, is guided by the goddess." He was talking slowly, making sure his words stuck. "She set you against the wall of thorns, and you have breached it. You have, as always, Laywren, overcome."

I glanced up at his eyes, willing to be convinced. It was so much easier to believe in fate than to be responsible for my mistake in judgment. A smile threatened the corners of his mouth as he read the slight release in the stubborn lines around my mouth.

He continued with certainty, "The reasons for getting into the District may not be known to us now, but we will understand the path when we have travelled it fully".

It was true. I could not always see the goddess' reasons, but that blindness did not mean reasons did not exist. I raised my chin and nodded. Dorn squeezed my shoulder encouragingly. Then, he started walking backwards toward the District.

"We will gather every item of food, every barrel of cider. Tell Cooks to prepare for a feast!" He waved his arm dramatically in the air. He turned and loped off.

Dorn was right. He was always right. We would celebrate as if this were a great victory. The Horde would be happy, even grateful to be led by me.

And then, we would move.

Chapter 9: Pledges Broken, Pledges Gained

One of Dorn's sayings, "Victory can wear defeat's cloak," did not come to my mind as members of the Horde presented me with their chosen. There were few captives of use from the District, but each would be expected to give the borh-hand—a pledge to the Horde in return for acceptance as wúsc-bearn.

In the midpoint of camp, I sat upon a temporary throne of piled logs and soft fur. The people of the Horde gathered—my people, peppering the air with their excited chatter and a renewed energy. These men and women hailed from different tribes, different lands. But they joined together under my rule to live a life of wandering, a life of warring in the goddess' name.

On my orders, the District had been emptied of every last piece of dried meat, every scrap of cloth, even every cooking pot. The mound of bounty from our conquest was piled in the heart of our encampment for all to see. I would not be honouring Grandfather's request by leaving food supplies for those who would stay in the District, for I had agreed to his surrender before I knew the well water was poisoned.

I looked to my left where the old man sat upon an upturned log. Grandfather had assured me his people were also suffering from an affliction of barrenness. His claim was supported by the fact that those in the District were mostly aging or old. Only one youth had been found. She was younger than any in the Horde, and she would be presented today. I was excited for I had yet to see her. But I was more excited about the knowledge Grandfather might have about the dark-skinned race.

The old man had feigned exhaustion, when I asked him about the seven we had captured. A small thrill of excitement wound its way in my guts. Soon, I would present Grandfather to Dorn. I felt he would enjoy having the old man's memories to journey through. And when my Warden presented me with the knowledge he discovered, it would take away the sting of his not knowing about the wall of wood.

Now, that we had the old warrior to question about the escaped serpent, the five captives hanging in the sacks were of no value. They would not be given the option to pledge. I ordered them slain.

A natural lull had started in the talk around me. I stood and like a ripple in water, heads turned my way. I raised my hand to speak, and the noise died out completely. I looked directly at many, meeting the eyes of those who trusted my lead. It was as Dorn had promised. The sense of victory was upon them.

I did not give a speech. It was not my way. Instead, I started the pledging.

"Who is blessed this day?" I called out.

Jendara stepped forward. She wore leather armour as I did, but her heart was softer. I had found her in the forests of Arisian, four years earlier. She was younger than I and had none of her kin with her in the Horde.

"I am blessed to have found a tender," Jendara said, gesturing to a small woman who knelt with her head down. Though the woman was not completely grey, she was not young either.

"She has agreed to care for me and my tent." Jendara looked at me anxiously, awaiting my decision.

I was concerned about the lack of water and taking on those we did not need. "Tenders grow old and can become a burden," I cautioned her, feeling she should know those who serve were not a luxury that could be supported by our roving life.

Jendara was quick to respond. "The woman can make weavings," she said, holding up a light-coloured cloth.

I motioned for her to bring it to me. The cloth lay delicately in my palm, its weave better than anything we had in the Horde. The softness of the fabric was enchanting against my rough fingers. I tucked the piece behind my chest armour, but I held my frown of disapproval.

Jendara nervously filled the silence, "I will care for her, when the time comes".

The warrior squared her shoulders to show me her determination. What I saw, though, was her loneliness. Her eyes pooled with a need for kin, reminding me of our state.

"Would you put down your sword to care for her?" I asked, testily.

"No, my Queen," Jendara knelt and bowed her head.

"When the woman can no longer care for herself, or be of use to the Horde, you will leave her." I made my decision and felt weak for it. Another decision I would not have made in the past.

"Yes, my Queen," Jendara kept her eyes cast down.

"Jendara of Arisian is blessed this day," I announced to the Horde.

There were a few mumbles of congratulations, and one man gave Jendara a friendly pat on the shoulder. I looked at the crowd and asked for the next to come forward.

Surprisingly, Dorn stepped into the clearing before me. He brought forward a young female of about six and ten years. She seemed frail and shaken, her eyes hidden behind straight black hair cut at mid cheek. His tanned hands looked dark against the white shoulders of the girl.

"I AM BLESSED TO HAVE found a chronicle ward," Dorn explained.

I blinked against the sudden burning in my eyes. I had expected the girl for word of her had spread quickly, but I had not expected Dorn to have her. I had seen Dorn return from the District, and he had not brought out a captive.

"Who cut the ties to her family?" I asked.

"I took her from the Nodurms," he said.

A small rustle went through the group. I was careful not to react, though I was shocked by Dorn's actions. This was not the way. I inclined my head to Kaj, leader of the Nodurms. I could tell by the darkening of Kaj's skin that he was not pleased. My heart's beat increased. Dorn's foolish actions were about to cause a ripple in the Horde's unity.

I gestured for Dorn to bring her closer, and he guided the young woman forward. I rose before her, feeling overly tall beside her slight build. Grabbing a handful of her long hair, I moved it aside to reveal her face. Her skin was translucent, and I could see the blood pulsing along the blue veins in her neck. By the marks on her throat, I knew the Nodurms had lost no time with her.

"Look here," I commanded, and she met my stare.

I skinned her eyes with my gaze, seeking to read her, but her eyes were guarded. I decided to use my medallion to test Dorn's theory.

"Saigim," I whispered.

In response, Lumen flipped through the girl's emotions, rippling her inner thoughts to revelation. I found the grief and loss of the conquered, the confusion of a girl-woman, the blackness of violation, and I found the tin of fear. More importantly, within her memory, there were stories suited to a chronicle ward, stories that held the history of her people.

Breaking the link, I flipped my cape back and settled on the fur hide. I knew Dorn spoke the truth, but the girl would have to prove her worth to the Horde. Leaning on my left arm, I gestured at her.

"Recount the battle," I instructed.

Her first words trembled on the hot air when she spoke. "We rose with the dawn, but you were already among us."

I nodded encouragingly. She lifted her chin and spoke louder.

"You came from the east... casting no shadow before you, and your war horn was the strangled cry of your first victim."

Her voice became stronger as she told the story to the silent people standing around her.

"Blood ran like a river on your blades, and the teeth of your hounds tore out the heart of the District. Your Queen was without mercy, mowing down our pride, as we had scythed wheat."

As she spoke, I considered her value against the threat she might pose to the Horde. If I allowed Dorn to keep her, the Nodurms would be vengeful. But if I left her with them, their games would waste her. Dorn said she was a chronicle ward. That meant her knowledge could save all of us. Dorn was not familiar with these lands and had to dig deep to find information that I could draw upon to lead the Horde.

The girl was young, but she would have begun training when she began to speak. The value of her memory was higher than grandfather's and should not be taken lightly. I looked at Dorn. He was listening intently comparing his chronicle to hers—two perspectives of the same event. The facts would be sound on both sides. The telling would be different.

The girl was also turning into a woman. I could see her young breasts pressing against her shift. And from Lumen's seek of her mind, I learned that she had bled during the last moon. Many of us had stopped bleeding long ago—when children had stopped being born. The girl's value to the Horde outweighed my gift of the old man, and the base needs of Kaj.

"You stacked our dead on the fields they had sown, but no seeds will grow following this harvest. The District is barren. Life has been denied us."

Her last word died out on the air, and she assumed the position of regard, kneeling before me.

I leaned forward on the throne. "What is done is past," I said.

The girl paused, as she searched her chronicles. Deep within her mind, she found the proper response. "Look to what is coming," she replied.

I was pleased. She carried proof of former contact with our people. I looked directly at Kaj but addressed the Horde as I said, "Dorn, the Chronicle Warden is blessed this day."

Kaj held my eye, while his face burned a dark red. The shock of his impudence rippled my tendons.

"Challenge?" I asked calmly and stood.

The word spread through the Horde like flames whispered in a field.

Kaj stared at me with hatred for the passing of three pulses. Then he said, "No," and bent low to touch his square-tipped fingers to the ground. "No challenge."

It was too late. Kaj had held my eye too long. Alive, he would be a danger to Dorn, and a disturbing force within the Horde. I released the clasp on my cape and moved forward into the clearing created by the groups' fluid movement outward.

"Challenge." I stated, my voice low.

Kaj rose, a sheen of sweat shining on his pronounced upper lip. The muscles in his hairy arms rippled as he removed his cape. His weapon of choice was a wide broadsword, the thick cross guard imbedded with rubies from his land. Each ruby, it was told, was a drop of blood from his ancestors.

Kaj's weight was his advantage with the sword, but he was slow. I laid my long sword aside and pulled my daggers from my thigh belts. Bending my knees into the Mantie pose, I began to circle.

Kaj moved in with wide, heavy strides, his flat feet kicking up red dust. He swung down with his sword, creating momentum with the stroke. I let him herd me, but my retreat was light, my steps dustless. For a second his left lung was exposed, but I did not jab. Then the sword came up at my chest, and I arched back allowing the blade to slip past my skin.

The weight of the sword pulled his arms up. His heart was exposed for the strike, but again, I did not jab.

He swung from the right, attempting to slice through my guts. I leapt back as the blade cut the air, then forward as his sword pulled him to the left, exposing his throat. My arms darted in with the Mantie snake strike and for a moment all movement stopped. Then Kaj staggered back, a shocked look in his eye, and his blood spurted high into the air.

The arching spray slapped the chronicle ward in the face as she moved forward, her eyes riveted on the death before her. Kaj fell heavily to his knees. Dropping his sword in the dust, he clutched his throat, as if trying to hold in his life. The moment held until his eyes rolled, and then he toppled.

Turning away from his sprawled body, I was surprised to see the girl standing so close to me, bloodlust shining in her eyes. She held her white smock clenched in her fist, the blood-spattered cloth wrinkling between her clawed fingers. Gone was the frightened, timid rabbit that had been presented to me.

I tapped Lumen into the Nodurms for their reaction to the loss of their leader. Already, they were arguing over who would get Kaj's sword. I looked to where the sword lay on the ground. The hard-cut rubies in the sword's handle shimmered like liquid. Then, the red drops ran from the sword, scurrying into the dust like centipedes in the forest. The ancestors had called back the drops of blood, for Kaj was the last of his line.

I walked to where Kaj had dropped his cloak. Wiping my daggers clean on the wool, I listened to the excited thrumming of the Horde around me. Sheathing my weapons, I turned and considered the crowd. Many struck their armour with their fists and their expressions showed acceptance of my justice. I paused before Kaj's wife, Nailia. She stood straight, her face void of emotion. She met my eyes without hesitation, and then she bowed.

I moved on.

When I came to Dorn standing by the chronicle ward, I was disturbed by the triumphant look in the girl's eyes. Dorn did not seem to notice the change. He was busy comforting the girl with a fatherly arm.

I looked intently at him. "Her life is yours—take it if you must," I said.

Dorn was too pleased to heed my warning.

Chapter 10: The Goddess Speaks

As night approached, a great fire was lit in the midpoint of camp where a meal fit for the Firslain had been laid. The dry heat broke, and the breeze cooled just enough to make us feel as if the air was worth breathing. The members of the Horde stood around the fire. All eyes were turned to me, and I held my back straight against the fatigue of the past few days.

"To the brave belong all things!" I called out, surprised at the strength in my voice.

The warriors roared their approval. I waited until the noise died.

"Your bravery has filled our table," I said gesturing to the food. "You have accepted those who would be your new kin and have welcomed them into the Horde."

Many nodded and those with wúsc-bearn patted them on arms and shoulders.

"Though our numbers do not grow, we hold steady." Some eyes slid from mine, followed by empty silence. I had poked at our greatest fear, and even I could see the need for more words.

"We hold steady," I repeated. "For in the heart of every man and woman of the Horde beats the strength of two." I struck my chest with my fist.

The thumping of arm guards on chests rose like a wave, then died when I raised my hand for silence.

"WE ARE NOT ALONE. THE District suffered as we do. But there are always answers, and the goddess will lead us to them." I smiled with reassurance.

Some seemed relieved at my words, willing to keep trusting, keep believing. I noted the brows that drew down, the eyes that looked away, the lips that tightened.

"Let the brave eat!" I called out to end the moment.

The Horde moved in on the food, a stream of leather and woolen-clad people, eager to fill their bellies and forget their woes. My hunger was upon me like thunder, but I stayed behind with Dorn and Rserker, and we echoed with emptiness until all had their food. Finally, we stepped forward to help ourselves to the newly slaughtered pig and lamb roasting on the open fire. There were tree fruits and roasted farce nuts, tubers from the ground and spices the cooks had never used before but had tampered with this day. I scooped food onto my plate with my bare hand as did every person before me.

Moving away from the table, I kicked a log onto its end, and sat down to relish the meat. Dorn and Rserker settled on either side of me. For long we gorged, not speaking. Grunting and chewing and swallowing, I felt my skin grow warm, and my eyes light up with new vigor.

Still, I did not attempt to speak over the din. I savored it, as I treasured the aftertaste of the spices. From my left, the new chronicle ward approached with her eyes downcast. She carried a tray of fruit cider in wooden mugs. Kneeling before me, the girl offered up a drink. Her attempt at humility rang false, and I hesitated, recalling her vindictive reaction to Kaj's death.

"It is the custom to trust," Dorn said quietly.

"It is my custom to live," I said.

Rserker broke into a hearty laugh that shook his thick frame, "And it is my custom to drink!" he roared, grabbing two mugs and drinking from both at the same time.

The cider ran down his beard, trickling behind his chain-mail shirt. Dorn laughed at his robustness and took the last mug, smiling at me over the rim.

I bit back a comment about waste. Rserker knew why I had paused before the mugs. Poison had been used to remove stronger Queen's than I from rule. And yet, he drank it, risking himself to reveal a threat to me. I looked at his hand wrapped around the cider mug and saw the glitter of a black pearl on his ring. I had given the ring to Rserker as a gift in recognition of his loyalty to me. The giving of the pearl had been easy. The taking of the pearl from the Gorkons had been more difficult and much more painful. My hand slid down to my thigh where the Gorkon's spear had pierced me. Thanks to Hinfūs, there was no scar, no ache—only a memory.

SEVEN YEARS EARLIER, we had challenged the Gorkons to battle. None pestered the Gorkons, but taking risks quenched the Horde's thirst for conquest, and I was young. And, the Gorkons had pearls.

The Gorkons were shaped like us, but had long, flat feet and slim one-jointed fingers that were webbed together with translucent skin. They lived on the coast in caves carved by the ocean's waves. Rarely did they come to land. They were always wet and slimy, except when they stayed out on the ocean rocks too long in the sun. They farmed black pearls and could not resist staring into the smooth orbs under the sun's heat. Some would become enchanted by the reflection in the round gems, gazing until the saltwater slime on their backs baked. Too long in the sun, and their black skin would crust and slough off. The worst of these pearl gazers looked like walking rot.

Rotting or no, they were gruesome to behold, but we were willing to look upon them to get to their treasure. The Gorkons did not hide their pearls in caves; they wore them pressed into their side fins. The fins hung down like broken wings from their waists ending in four little hollow tubes of skin that could wrap and hold a pearl like a sock holds feet. The bigger the pearls in the fins, the more respected the Gorkon.

We could not fight them in the water, or in the caves. We needed to have the advantage of solid land. So, we had captured a young one, and its fearful cries had brought the brutes to shore.

My back had chilled with fear in the morning sun, when those slogging beasts dragged their legs through the shallows to reach us. They carried spears made of sharp coral and rock slings that could fling sea urchins at bow speed. But their battle of choice was hand-to-hand combat. No human hands could hold their slippery limbs or long grip their unanchored skin.

Our archers hit them with a volley when they were still knee-deep. Most of the Gorkons showed no reaction to the arrows. They felt little pain, much like fish.

Our plan was to cut the fins from the beasts with our long swords, but it was not easy. The fins were soft and swung from front to back as the Gorkons moved. I spotted one with immense sagging side fins. Running to it, I got its attention with a slice to its sagging belly. It tried to grab me, but I kept my feet moving, ducking its arms and dashing in at the fin. The sand caved under my feet and dancing from my enemy's reach became more difficult with each passing minute. I twisted from a spear jab and spotted my chance. Slicing upward, I caught the fin with my blade, close to the beast's side. The fin ripped free and flew into the air, spinning end over end with the weight of the pearls.

The Gorkon croaked in rage as it sprang away, ignoring me now that its pearls were hewn from its side. It ran clumsily across the sand, scrambling in blind greed for its status stones. I raced after the creature to cut off its other fin, not seeing a new Gorkon rise silently from the sea, behind me.

Just as the injured creature turned to face my attack, a spear flew from behind and felled me in mid-step. The shaft shook my bones as it drove into my thigh, the force pushing me chin first to the feet of my enemy. I sent out a siren on Lumen and felt Rserker's immediate reply through my medallion.

~ I pledge this heart that beats, these lungs that breath, this mind that thinks to thee ~

I swung my pierced leg over and twisted onto my back. The pain flashed brighter than the sun, but even blinded, I met the beast's sling with my blade. Sand from the blow filled my eyes. The Gorkon stepped on my sword arm with his cold, flat foot, holding it to the ground.

~ Rserker! ~

Through my watering eyes, I could see the Gorkon from the sea moving closer. Soon I would have two on me. Pulling my short dagger, I sliced up at the Gorkon's calf. It let out a grunt falling back away from my arm. Pain would not stop it, but it knew where its tendons were. I tried rolling up onto my feet, but the spear handle dug into the ground, the point pushing me into a moment of blackness.

~ And while there is breath and beat and thought, I pledge all to my Queen ~

The second Gorkon fell on me, his shagging skin, cold and wet. The agony of the spear was pushing me in and out of a dark shower of white sparks. I could feel the fin pearls, cool against my side as the Gorkon began to wrap me in a suffocating hold.

~ Rserker ~

This time, my warrior brother did not answer me through Lumen. Instead, I heard the pounding of his feet, the whistle of his slicing blade, and then there had been nothing but dead silence.

RSERKER'S LAUGH BROUGHT me back to the present and the fire. From the sounds surrounding the night, the members of the Horde had released themselves to celebrate. I watched the twisting legs, the leaping backs as a few danced around the pile of blazing logs.

As warriors do, Dorn and Rserker were sharing their tales of the District conquest. They hadn't noticed my lapse into the past, and they didn't notice when I walked softly past the sway of the flames.

Pulling on my hood, I hid my face beneath it. Cloaked, I could move among my people, basking in their camaraderie without the crust of reverence. The smell of sweat and burned meat blended with the breath of cider on full stomachs. I could hear a man talking loudly, confident and brass. Occasionally, a voice shrieked or argued. I moved outside of the circle, away from the thick scent of the fire smoke.

Here in the dark, the Julees spoke softly among themselves as they tended the animals at the outer edge of the camp. They were a quiet people, more interested in caring for herds than being among their own kind. Beyond, I could see the black shapes of the hounds as they snapped and yipped, gathering for their nightly hunt. I moved further still, out to where the guards walked the red soil, or hunkered in the trees, keeping watch.

The song of the Horde followed me, all the sounds of a community rich with emotion and life. Yet, empty. No babe cried, no youth entertained with somersaults, or questioned and learned.

Sorrow pulled at my mouth, drawing down the corners. The Horde was drained. I put my hand to my stomach—a board of tight muscle that held my body together like reeds formed a basket. And there I stood and sighed, until the scent of sage floated to my senses. Sage—the sacred herb of Goddess.

Curious, I walked back toward the camp, invisible in the dark. Just past the animals, a lighter shadow stirred by a small fire. Nethaz was drawing water from the barrel reserves. He bent and his armour bands of brown leather tightened across his broad back. I stopped outside of the fire's light and watched the giant in silence. Nethaz turned and looked blindly in my direction. He was unable to see me in the dark, for few had my vision.

Assured he was unobserved, Nethaz stood straight, his elbow high, and drank from the mug.

When I entered the light from his fire, I spoke. "The wind does not burn, tonight."

He slowly lowered the mug from his wet lips. "A welcome change."

His blue eyes sought mine beneath my hood. I slipped it back off my hair, and we stood for a moment, taking in the sight of each other. His high forehead was circled by a blue ribbon of cloth that snaked into the plait of his shiny, black hair. The single braid hung down over his shoulder, as thick as my arm.

Flaring my nostrils, I drew in the air between us.

"You scent the air with the goddess' breath," I said. "Was she whispering to you?"

"My ears are not worthy of the goddess," he replied.

We had left our conversation on the hill, but I was ready to begin again. "Then, how do you know the Firslain bar the return from the hall?"

He wiped the rim of his mug on his forearm and handed it to me. I let him hold it in mid-air, waiting for an answer. He stared at me in silence.

I was not used to being disobeyed. To hide my anger, I took the cup from his hand. Turning my back to him, I walked to the water barrel and twisted the spout roughly. A trickle of lukewarm water filled the mug.

"I do not have the words to tell you," he whispered behind me.

I did not turn around as I drank from the mug, showing him my displeasure.

He kept his voice soft as he continued. "I traveled for a year, looking for those who served the goddess. Before I found the Horde, there was only empty land, and dark creatures who would rule it."

THE GROUND SHIFTED, and I braced my legs to steady myself.

"If you would allow me," Nethaz stepped forward, closing the space between his chest and my back, "I can show you."

The water barrels rippled in the air before me, and I knew enchantment was at work. From behind, Nethaz slid his thick arm past my ribs and wrapped his wide hand over mine around the mug. Every muscle in my body tensed at his closeness, but I held myself still for his revelation.

"It does not matter that the mug is full if it is not brought to your lips."

He gently pulled me back until I rested against him. The muscles in his chest pressed against my shoulders, his skin cooler than the night. I shifted my feet, uncomfortable within his hold, but unwilling to break the strange mood I found myself caught in. The giant took a deep breath and pressed his lips to the side of my hair.

"Each death," he started. "Each death takes us closer to the end of our time."

Nethaz moved his arm in a small circle, his forearm rubbing against the side of my breast. My eyes were drawn to the water inside the mug, which swirled in black and silver rings. His lips near my ear, Nethaz began to hum. As the humming grew louder it swelled in my chest like the buzzing of sting-ants. Strangely, I wanted to turn and press my face into his chest. But, Nethaz cupped his hand around the side of my head, one thick finger beneath my chin, and tilted my sight back to the cup. Then, I heard the goddess whisper.

In the swirling water of the mug, I saw a toothless mouth. The lips seemed frozen in a gag as darting flashes of silver turned in an endless circle within the black maw. The lips of the mouth stretched as thin as a woman before a babe's head crowns. Then, a great press from within forced them to swell as if ready to spew all into the night. But the flashes of silver light could not pass, for barring the way out of the gape were two spinning blades—battle axes so large, only a giant or a curse could wield them. Nethaz's hot breath burned in my ear, carrying the faint cries of the souls trapped behind the blades. It was as if they lived within his lungs and called out to me, begging for release, pleading for a saviour. My knees buckled, and I fell deeper into Nethaz's trance.

"You must tip the womb and spill them out," he whispered.

His arm stopped swirling the mug, but he held my hand to it, still. His other arm wrapped around my stomach, and he leaned over, bending my body with his. As we bent, my eyes never left the mug. Even as my breath was pressed out and my insides felt crushed by his weight, still I watched the water trickle to the lip of the cup and spill the silver darts onto the dust. They scurried like minnows without a stream. I reached down to scoop them back into the cup when the sound of the Horde's merrymaking burst through the vision.

Twisting out of Nethaz's grasp, I slipped into the darker shadow of the water wagon. The wood of the wagon felt hard and empty against my back. Nethaz moved to stand beside me and I resisted the urge to enter his arms and the vision again. Instead, I stood and breathed deeply, sucking the scent of sage and man-sweat deep into my lungs to calm my spinning thoughts.

The goddess had clearly sent me a message, had clearly chosen a path for me. She had spoken through the giant, and I would heed her command. Now I knew the truth about the cycle. Now I could act. In silence, Nethaz and I stood, side by side, looking out into the night. A wind picked up from the south and brushed my skin. It was hot and drew the moisture from my skin. The reprieve was over.

Chapter 11: A New Dawn Surrenders

I awoke to a warning bark from my hound. Opening my eyes without moving, I found myself face to muzzle with Hinfūs who was growling low in his throat. I sat up quickly and looked around the tent. We were alone. The flanks were standing guard outside, the sun outlining their strangely shaped bodies against the tent walls.

"What is wrong with you, Hound?" I croaked, taking in his lowered head and flattened ears.

I pushed at his chest to move him back, then groaned with surprise at the stiffness plaguing my body. It was difficult to stand, but stand, I did. My lips and throat felt dusted. I could barely swallow. Fumbling the water skin to my mouth, I drew deep, then placed it to my forehead, I rubbed the dampness onto my face.

Hinfūs crawled towards me on his belly and began licking my feet. My woolen shirt was soaked with sweat. I peeled it off my body and tossed it at my hound.

"Begone!"

Thinking I may have caught a fever from the District people, added chills to my sweating skin. A drop of precious moisture ran down between my breasts, intent on reaching my birth-knot. I picked up the soft cloth woven by Jendara's tender and used it to wipe the sweat from my neck and chest.

That's when I saw the marks on my shoulder. Bright reds and pink swirls that marked my skin with the glow of a sunset. My mind froze as I witnessed that which I had never thought to see.

"The flush . . ." I whispered in awe through my cracked lips.

It had been so long since any woman had flushed, that I had never seen the marks before. But I had heard how the flush would look on a woman who was ripe to make a child, and these marks on my skin were much like those in the tales. The idea that I might flush, that any woman after fourteen years of barrenness might flush, stunned me into immobility.

Hinfūs was back at my ankles, licking my skin with his hot tongue. His attentions were abnormal and unwanted. He wasn't trying to heal the wound in my side, for it had knit.

"Get away!" I slapped at him.

I turned my head to take another look at the flush marks on my shoulders. It was hard to see in the tent's light, but I didn't want to walk out into the day's light, yet. I wasn't ready to show my condition.

According to tradition, I should announce my state to the Horde for it would be up to the flush to choose my mate. I had never experienced it but had heard the mate choosing was irrevocable. Like all people, I had never questioned my lack of choice in who would sire my child. It was the way things were and had been for millennia. The only question had been whether I would experience the flush before I passed out of childbearing years.

But now, things were not as they once were. If Nethaz was to be believed, the Firslain had betrayed their mother, our mother—Goddess. I wasn't going to trust the old ways when they were under siege. Especially, not after the vision Nethaz had shown me of the trapped souls. This was too important. I had to make the right decision.

I pulled on my woolen shirt, making sure the red patterns on my skin were covered and then left my tent, seeking Dorn.

As I moved through camp, the sound of the flanks wiry thigh hairs rubbing together kept rhythm with my steps. Normally, others shied away from me when I was with my guards. But this morning, my people showed their respect by stopping their tasks and tipping their heads.

Yesterday's victory was evident, and so was cider-fugue. The warriors groaned or laughed, depending on their state. I tipped my head to each man and woman I passed, warriors who had risked their lives to take the District. Their loyalty was strong. Dorn had been right to argue for a celebration of our conquest. He was always right, and that is why I needed him now.

My heart skipped a beat when I came around a tent and saw Nethaz. He stood out from the group of men he was talking with, rising above the tallest warriors. The giant sensed my approach and turned, then dropped his eyes in a show of deference. I paused in front of him, wondering if he and his vision had caused me to wake with the flush. Nethaz stepped to the side to block the sun with his head and ease my looking up at him.

"Good morn," I said peering at him with suspicion.

The other warriors moved out of earshot but kept us in their sight.

"Good morn," Nethaz bowed, the sun bursting into a golden haze around his head.

"Has the morning brought you any new revelations?" I asked, warily.

The giant smiled down at me and in a low voice said, "I was curious about something. Thinking about something..."

"Speak then." I shifted my weight onto my other foot. I had no time for repeated sentences.

"I was thinking about the District tender—the woman who was presented to you by Jendara?"

"What about her?" I watched two Horde members walk past, carrying their tent-bag and other belongings. They turned their heads away to give our conversation privacy in the busy camp.

"Would you really command the young warrior to leave the old woman to her death?" he asked.

I frowned at his foolish question. "The old hang onto souls that could start anew. Why would we delay a glorious rebirth?" I asked him.

"To respect the body the soul has grown to know," Nethaz answered. His blue eyes were darker today, more shadowed.

My heart sped up. Nethaz and his ideas always upset my body's rhythms. "The body is but a vessel. The soul is the true source of life."

"And the old man you took from the District," he asked. "Will you leave him behind as well?"

"When I am finished with the old man, I will leave him behind, and he will end his journey by releasing a soul to the Hall," I bit off each word with impatience. But the last word hung in my mouth like sour fruit. Release a soul to the Hall that imprisoned souls. Damn the giant!

"Kneel!" I commanded.

It was time for me to truly explore the roots of his heretic thoughts. Nethaz knelt upon one knee, turning his eyes to the ground. I cupped his clean-shaven chin. It filled my hand. Tilting his head up, I looked deep within his round orbs, searching the mind that could raise a vision quest from the goddess. I turned on Lumen with a thought-touch.

"Saigim," I ordered it to flip through Nethaz's motives, desires and regrets like a red crawler flicks under rocks.

Not once during my seek did Nethaz blink. I found his honour-bond to the goddess. It was strong and unquestionable. I also found his mind reflecting on the heat from my hand. I pulled it away from his chin.

As I sought his thoughts, I felt him looking for mine. Never had I sensed this from a member of the Horde. I was able to block his gentle probing easily, but still... I pulled away before I was finished, shutting down the bridge between us. I was puzzled, and now, warier of Nethaz. He did not wear a Lumen, yet he was able to flicker within my mind. Throughout the seek, the giant's expression had not changed. He continued to look up at me, with serene honesty—his hand resting on his knee without threat.

This close to him, I could see the blue in his eyes was spun like ribbons. The pattern created a mesmerizing swirl that enticed my gaze. I felt a light tickle on my breast. As the sensation grew, I brushed it away, thinking it was a bug. But then, the buzzing melted across my skin, and I felt a flowing within. An internal movement of my blood as if I was pulled by a tide and Nethaz was the moon. I staggered, and the giant put out a hand to catch me but was shrewd enough not to touch me.

From deep within my instinct, rose the understanding that the flush was choosing my mate.

"No!" I did not mean to call out the word, but it burst from my lips in a shout. The flanks responded, hissing at the giant with threat.

Nethaz frowned in confusion and started to stand, his hand still hovering in the air between us. I became aware of the other male warriors' interest in our little scene. It was time to leave.

I altered my expression to appear satisfied. Then, without a word, I continued walking through camp. The bind holding me to Nethaz felt like hooks in my back. I imagined them stretching out behind me, pulling my skin from my bones. I quickened my pace, casting a glance over my shoulder to find the giant watching my retreat. I wondered if he could sense the flush.

I had to question how the flush, the instrument of Goddess' cycle, could choose a giant to be my mate. It did not bear thinking. To me, this error, this unthinkable union was more evidence of the cycle's worsening state.

Passing the cook's fire, I saw Rserker shoving the last of his breakfast into his mouth. He raised his hand in greeting.

I was breathless, unable to speak the expected greeting. To cover my awkwardness, I reached into the cook's pot and lifted out a scoop of gruel on my fingers.

"It is a fine morning when greeted with a full belly and a plan for travel," Rserker pulled the back of his arm across his beard, clearing it of food scraps.

Cook ran up and offered me a plate of the morning stew. I sucked my fingers clean and waved her away. She stepped back from me but stood looking eagerly at the flanks. Someday, she would probably dare to roast them.

"Take your thoughts from my guards, lest they lead you to suffering," I warned the old hag.

She shrieked and ran off to join the other two cooks. I watched them huddle and snivel together. Rserker laughed at the little scene. I was heartened by Cook's fearful reaction.

"What would you have me do in preparation for travel?" Rserker asked.

The revelation of the axe-bound Hall and Nethaz's questions had begun their work on me. I reconsidered my decision to refuse Grandfather's surrender condition. Letting the old die in the District would not guarantee a quick return for those souls. Still, it was not my duty to keep the conquered alive. More and more, I needed Dorn's counsel.

"Rserker, have Nethaz cut out one week's worth of supplies for those who are staying in the District. Remind him that the best is for the Horde."

Rserker grinned like an imp, "Shall I have him take back bread."

I forced a laugh. "Yes, but only a few loaves, and only those with gruel worm and mold. I would eat the rest."

Rserker tossed back his head and laughed deep and long.

I was pleased at his good cheer and felt a little less shaky. "Have the giant move the old grandfather in with him," I said. "Dorn will not need the old man's tales, now that he has the chronicle ward."

"Yes," Rserker grinned. "Dorn will enjoy plucking her mind, as much he enjoys plucking her flower."

I turned and walked away from Rserker's leer before he could say anymore. Rserker's words disturbed me. I had wanted to share the news of the flush with Dorn. Perhaps even ... I bit my lip to sharpen my mind.

I was still frowning slightly, when I came to the area where Dorn's tent was set up. The three wards were sitting upon the ground, listening to Dorn's words. The two males had been with us for over a year. Only the District girl was new, and she was the youngest. Dorn was moving among them, pacing as he spoke, his red cape swinging with his movements. I paused in my approach to listen. Tapping Lumen, I silently dismissed the flanks and turned my attention to Dorn's voice.

"You are the record. You will keep alive the legends of others, making sure that none forget those who have earned a place in your memory." Dorn gazed sternly at the wards.

I watched his chest rising with the words, pressing out against the leather bands that crossed over his smooth muscles.

"You will sing the songs of warriors, leaders and the goddess." He paused, as only Dorn can. Then, he turned and looked down on the wards. "But, none will sing of you."

Dorn's gaze traveled across the attentive faces to pause at the girl from the District. "The breath you seize will not serve your life, it will serve the tale as it whirls in the air before you."

The girl had been sitting on her knees, but as Dorn focused on her, she tensed her thigh muscles, raising herself slightly.

"It will be your task to adorn truth but never change it." He walked closer to the girl, and her eyes brightened above her delicate features. "It will be your duty to remember the deeds and to raise up the legends."

The wind blew Dorn's wavy, brown hair back from his brow. I studied his face, drawn to the mind behind the eyes. I too was entranced by the words on his lips. As taken with his speech as the girl was. He could recount any battle, telling a tale to lift the heart of every warrior. The task of the Chronicle Warden was a calling, and Dorn had spent his years practicing his craft, seeking out legends, listening to the elders, retelling every event he witnessed.

As I gazed at him, I realized he had been with the Horde for more than eight years, and in that time, he had stored every achievement I had made, every victory I had led, every bounty I had taken. In all these years, Dorn had never tried to court me. Not even when we had first met in the town of Dunveegan.

IN DUNVEEGAN, THERE had been a place of words—a building where tales had been stored on animal hides. The town had become the target of many peoples' curiosity, and they travelled far to see the stories in writing. Dunveegan was one of the few places where homes lined a street and wares were sold out of buildings instead of in an open market. We had heard of the crowds migrating to the town, and I knew we could find something of gain. I did not know then, that the treasure we sought was Dorn.

I had been a leader for a short time, but my choices, my courage, my gift for finding adventure had bound the oath of seven warriors to me. We moved down the street of the town in the dead of night. We were an alarming sight of weapons and armour, of mixed tribe and free spirit. I did not like walking between the two rows of buildings that lined the street. Towns were not for me, for the streets' households blocked my view and my escape. As we edged closer to the centre of town, loud voices and snippets of song floated on the night air. One of the buildings leaked yellow light around its ill-fitting doors.

Rserker and I went in alone to test the welcome. The rest of our group moved to stand outside the building, taking posts that would give us advantage should the night end in contest.

I paused just inside the doors, adjusting my eyes to the dim light of flickering candles and rusty oil torches. The walls were unpainted wood, beams and slats ending on a packed dirt floor. Tables were squares of timber with logs for legs, surrounded by travelers, drinkers. A few tables were tipped over and beneath one was the still figure of a man. Dead or drunk, I could not tell.

I wrinkled my nose at the rank smell of unwashed skin and the sharp smoke of sweet reed. A few eyes slid our way, but we were mostly ignored—a good sign, for I preferred to move unnoticed.

Reserker walked to a long wooden counter held up by cider barrels. I scanned the room again, before I left the safety of the doorway. I could see none who lived by the sword. Most of the men and women were here to drink cider and share their wants, their diseases. A woman laughed, her mouth a brown rim of rotting teeth. The man beside her pushed his bearded lips onto hers, bending her neck, roughly. She came up for air, her price on her tongue.

I released my sword pommel and wiped the sweat from my palm onto my thigh. The airless room was heavy with moisture. Satisfied the crowd held little threat, I moved to stand with Rserker who was already ordering a drink.

A bald, fat man watched me walk up with a greasy smile. His glance raked my body from head to toe. I narrowed my eyes at him, as he scratched beneath his apron.

"Bounty hunters?" he asked nodding at the blades snug in sheaths on my thighs.

I frowned at his black, piggish eyes and said nothing.

"Seekers of the sights," Rserker answered with a smile and bowed, drawing the pig man's gaze away from me.

The black eyes returned to my face as the man licked his chapped lips and answered, "We have sights that will make your blood curdle with fear."

Then, he smiled slickly at Rserker, "Or boil with lust."

A woman shrieked behind me. I wanted a wall for my back.

The fat man hawked up some phlegm and spit it near his feet. I followed the path to his grimy toe sticking out from the worn leather of his shoe.

"All comes for a price," he bargained.

I knew this was where we were supposed to reach for our money bags, but Rserker and I were too smart to let the thieves in the room know where we kept our coin.

"Lust you say?" Reserker grinned and fingered his trimmed beard. A blonde who was beautiful once, left the lap of a drunken fool and swayed closer to us.

The fat man laughed.

I looked through the room again, adding up the cider mugs, looking at the clothes of the people. This rabble had little we would want. As Rserker moved towards the blonde, I decided to go outside and allow one of the others to enter. I would breathe better in the night air.

I turned to leave, but a steady voice at my side drew my attention.

"There is room at my table, if you wish."

In front of me stood a man. A man who stood out from the others. He had a handsome face framed by long, wavy, light brown hair. And he was looking at me with honest interest instead of the leer most of the other men wore. Dressed in a clean tunic and leather leggings, he carried a sword, but not the edge of a warrior. I held my place and my tongue.

"Away from the noise," his hand was out, pointing to a table behind a half wall, hidden from the curious eyes of the strangers.

He smiled soothingly, revealing healthy teeth. "You are welcome to join me."

His eyes were open, friendly, intelligent eyes. The fat man was still talking, trying to offer me one of his women.

"Cider," I growled at the pig man.

Then, I lifted my chin at the table, deciding to stay. Following the stranger, I watched his walk. His back was straight, and his stride was confident. I could see by the tunic's stretch that he was lean and fit beneath it. Behind the half wall, the stranger slid over a wooden bench polished by years of seated patrons. I stayed standing, looking around the private seating area. He casually laid his hand on the table and waited patiently. His hands were clean, the nails trimmed.

When the pig had brought me a cider, when I had paid, when the pig man had returned to the counter, I cautiously sat down on the bench. But I kept one thigh on the outer edge of the seat, my foot plant-ed flat on the floor. A welcome burning followed the cider's path down my throat.

Finally, the stranger spoke. "You are a traveler?"

I was not ready to talk, but the cider's heat loosened the muscles in my tongue.

"Yes," I answered.

"And you are well-armed," he said, looking at my sword, my dag-gers.

I frowned at him and put down the mug, "The better to slay those who would interfere with me and mine."

He nodded, "I could tell you were the leader." His eyes glowed with interest.

"What is it you want?" The candle flickered away from my breath, for I spoke roughly.

"Your story," he replied, as if it were the most natural thing to ask for.

It was an answer that flattered my pride. But, I could give little of myself, could talk little of myself.

"My story is my own." I surprised myself by letting out a long sigh.

I hadn't meant to sigh, but it had come out, had been called out by the man's alluring presence, tempting me to share. I sat up straighter and looked more closely at him, wondering if he were enchanting me. I took in his relaxed posture, the turn of his shoulders, and his attentive expression. He was purposefully holding himself to invite talk. I was suddenly aware of the contrast between us.

I was straight-backed and tense, leaning away from him, keeping my attention on the room. He had slipped in behind the half wall, able to hide behind it, but I had to stay alert, always ready to run, always pre-pared to fight.

"Perhaps you will enjoy listening, then," he said without rancor.

His eyes were soft, open to sharing, the corners crinkling with a promise of humour.

My eyes were half-hooded with heavy lids, the dark orbs glittering with reflection—a closed door to those who would read me. I took another gulp of cider. I had time before Rserker would be ready to leave. Turning in my seat to face him, I left the distractions of the room behind.

"Speak."

"Do you know the Wells of Westeenian?" he asked me, reaching for his quart of cider and offering to fill my glass. I pushed my mug closer to him.

"No," I answered, wondering if the drink would be drugged.

"So, you have not heard of the Wishes of Trush?"

I held my newly-filled mug under my nose and inhaled a little steam. Mind-touching Lumen, I had the disc check the draught. It was safe. I lifted the edge of the wooden mug to my lips, continuing to stare at the amber eyes awaiting my response.

He leaned closer to me and whispered as if confiding a secret. "It is said, if you walk to the wells from the west, and speak your wishes to the depths, your desires will come true." He leaned back against the smoke-stained wall, watching for my reaction. His movement left the scent of pine behind to tickle my nose.

I put down the mug, my mind beginning to turn on a new adventure. "How far are these wells?"

"It's hard to say," he shrugged. "I know the way but have not walked the path."

"So, you are a guide?" I asked. This was an invitation for him to share his name. I was interested, now that I could see his use.

He sat up straighter, turning to face me as square on as the table would allow. "I am Dorn, Chronicle Warden for the Eldersleens."

"A tale tracker," I used the common name for his kind.

"If you wish," Dorn answered good-naturedly, spreading his hands in the air.

"Why are you not with your people?" I questioned him, suspicious.

"Tales are best gathered through travel."

"Traveling alone can be dangerous."

"Finding a group to align with can be difficult," Dorn replied.

My eyes dropped to his hip, where his sword was sheathed in leather. "Can you use your weapon?" I asked.

"When I need to," he smiled.

Now it was his turn. His eyes took in my traveling cape.

"Do you journey far?" he asked.

I had decided he would be of use to our group. I took my hand from the mug and leaned back, finally open to speaking with him.

"We seek that which we do not grow tired of. The horizon calls to us, and we follow. The wind spins our course, and we turn. The path is never too long," I said.

My lips curved in appreciation of my own words.

The man's attention was drawn to my mouth, but his tone was serious when he replied. "The horizon is the backdrop to destiny," he lifted his glance to mine. "But the wind can confuse the strongest purpose."

I did not answer, for I could see he was wise, and he had more to say.

"I carry a thousand tales of places and people," he smiled, "and bounty."

I frowned at his reference. The title of bounty hunter did not rest lightly on my conscience.

Dorn continued, "The map is in my head. The journey lies in my heart."

He put out his hand, and I looked at the work-roughened palm. I pressed my hand into his and squeezed an agreement against the warmth of his skin.

"I am Laywren, and I lead the Horde," I said with pride.

I had been trying to think of a name for my group of fighters and now it was done. Dorn's brows had shot up with curiosity, and I released a true smile to shine through my normally closed features. Rserker met Dorn when he had emerged from his dalliance with the blonde woman. We spent the night plotting the next adventure and drinking cider.

A few days later, we had finished taking what we needed in the town of Dunveegan, Dorn had pleaded with me not to torch the building that held the story hides. I had granted him this first request, and later learned the hides were under the protection of the RaiMen Empirees. Those soldiers would have hunted us down and slaughtered us like dogs, if we had not listened to Dorn.

EIGHT YEARS LATER, Dorn was still giving me sound advice. And though he was always aware of me, always attentive to my presence, he had never courted me. I knew Dorn walked with me because I made history, and I had thought that was good enough for him, until he had kissed my hand.

I shifted on my feet, growing stiff watching Dorn instruct the wards. He looked down at the young girl, flattered by her attention, as I was often flattered by his.

"You do not live for your life. You live to record the lives of others. You are the record," he smiled into the girl's eyes.

The wards were enthralled. I blew a little air out of my nostrils at the display. The sound caught Dorn's attention, and he turned and met my eye. He smiled, deepening the creases at the sides of his mouth. Stepping past the wards, he walked up to me.

"In which direction will you lead us?" He asked, his gaze traveling over my face. My skin warmed under his study.

"North." Out of the corner of my eye, I saw the chronicle ward narrow her eyes at us.

"This is good," Dorn nodded, "I have tales of the North."

The sun slipped behind the brown of his eyes making them glow like sap stones.

"How was the night?" I asked. "Did the captive wail for her loss?"

His skin reddened slightly, and I glanced at the girl to catch her reaction. She was standing, her head cocked in our direction trying to hear.

"Go. Prepare to travel," Dorn waved his hands at the wards, and they moved away, taking the girl with them.

As Dorn turned back to me, a burst of hot wind drove the tangled hair off my neck, baring my skin to the sun. I saw the pulse jump in his throat.

"Laywren," Dorn's eyes widened as he whispered my name in wonder.

Reaching forward, he made as if to brush the skin at the hollow of my throat with his thumb. I stepped back, holding my face blank as I read his emotions.

His voice broke when he spoke. "Laywren? Can it be?"

I was afraid to say it out loud, "I'm not sure."

"May I look?" Dorn asked.

I nodded, and he moved to my back, lifting my hair from my shoulders. I could not see the back of my neck, so I tapped Lumen to look through Dorn's eyes. The curve of my neck appeared in my mind, fading out the camp before me. I watched Dorn's thumb rub against my reddened skin. Under his hand, the blood rose up creating a pattern of pink swirls, ever so faint. Oddly, the markings were not as sharp as they had been in the morning.

I drew my sight from Lumen and pulled my woolen tunic away from my shoulder. The flush was gone from there. Confused, I stepped away from Dorn, and placed my hand against my neck. I was not ready for him to see, for I could not be sure.

"It is the flush!" Dorn said definitively, moving to stand in front of me. His eyes glittered with excitement.

I looked away from him and shook my head.

"Laywren!" A small laugh burst through his lips and the delight in his voice made my stomach flutter. "This is a blessing!"

When I did not respond, he stepped forward, cupping my chin in his hand and lifting my eyes to his. I reached up and removed his hand from my face, frowning at his forwardness.

"We must not make a false claim." I was suddenly afraid that what I had wished for was coming true.

Dorn's mouth dropped open in disbelief at my reaction. But then he sighed and nodded, suddenly somber and respectful.

"You should see Cook," he decided.

I was disappointed. I had expected a different reaction. The faintest shadow flickered behind his lashes, and I was tempted to use Lumen on him to see how he had spent his night.

Instead I left him, walking quickly in the direction of Cook's fire, but after passing a few tents, I changed course and went to my own. My emotions were heightened, making me feel out of control. What was I doing worrying about Dorn and that slip of a girl? I had a Horde to command!

I sent out a message through Lumen to the warriors who were tracking the serpent. They had not returned, and now that we were ready to move, I would have to keep in contact with them. The group responded that they were three days North, at the base of a mountain. I could see the mountain's peak from where I stood, small under the clouds. We would leave in the morning, and I announced this to everyone in the Horde using Lumen. Within weeks we would meet up with the others, and then I would take up the hunt for the escaped captive.

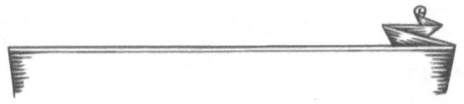

Chapter 12: My Rule for a Man

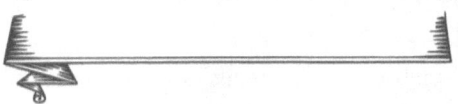

The moment I entered the tent, the flanks reacted. They clicked and clacked in the corner, waking Hinfūs. He whined and crawled to my side, sniffing my crotch. Slapping his head away, I commanded the hound to leave me. I moved to the back corner of the tent that held my weapons to escape the bluster. Drawing my long sword, I hefted its weight.

"This," I spoke aloud, "holds no surprise. I know the arc of my swing, the steadiness of my strike, the bite of the blade."

I ran my hand lightly down the side of the cutting edge, admiring the sheen in the dimmed light of the tent. Hinfūs sniffed me again, and whined, licking randomly at my hand and thigh.

"Be gone, slatherer!" I shoved the hound away with my foot, pointing my finger at my side to show the unscarred knit in my skin. "I am healed!"

Dorn's tread outside of my tent caught my attention. I heard him hesitate, and then pace around the entrance.

"Laywren," he called impatiently. "May I enter?"

I did not answer. The flanks rolled their yellow eyes at each other, excited at the emotions sparking the air. I quietly put down my sword. I heard him sigh deeply as he waited, then he started to move away. Suddenly needing him more than I wished to avoid him, I motioned to Right Flank to open the tent.

Dorn entered, but stayed standing in the tent's flap. He ruffled his hair with his hand, and the waves fell to curl softly under his jaw line. His face held heated frustration.

"Dorn," I warned.

The tent closed behind him, shutting out the sun's light. I stepped back.

"Laywren, I wish to speak freely." He was more serious than I had ever seen him.

I was cautious to leave the safety of my rank, but I wanted to hear what he would say. I wanted to know what he would do.

"I free you to speak," I said, my voice breaking on the words that would remove the boundary of my status.

Dorn stepped closer to me, and I veiled my thoughts.

"Why did you not see Cook?" he asked, angrily.

I turned my face away and a thousand reasons tumbled into my mind. How could I show my neck to Cook? If I had the flush, I would have to announce it to the Horde. If I announced the flush, everything would be delayed, and the men in the North were waiting. My desire to kill the escaped captive was strong, stronger than my need to participate in a festival of the flush that could last days. If I announced the flush, I would have to obey the flush's choice, one guided by the goddess. Or so I used to think. Perhaps the choice was guided by the Firslain. Or Nethaz! At this point, I could not trust the old ways to choose my mate. I could not trust the old traditions. And what if the flush was false? Then, some would suspect disfavour. My rule would be questioned.

Dorn interrupted my thoughts by grabbing my shoulders, "For Goddess' sake, answer me!"

I twisted out of his grip, my hand going to the dagger at my thigh. "I have not chosen this path," I said, my chin high.

His brows came down hard over his eyes. "The flush chooses!"

"I will choose!" I pushed my face into Dorn's space.

"How dare you place yourself above the goddess."

I held my ground, stung by his words into silence. The flanks stamped their hooves in the dust behind me, warning Dorn.

His voice was cold as he continued. "This is not about you. Should you defy the traditions of our people ... Should you disregard the ritual of the goddess, how will that affect everything that holds this life together? Your contempt will destroy the fabric we weave to keep you Queen!"

Never had he spoken to me like this. Never would I have let it happen. My breath left me slowly as I stood at my full height and looked down my nose at him. "*You* keep me Queen? You, tale tracker? I was Queen long before you became servant to my rule."

Dorn's anger faded before my words, the sides of his mouth turning down in resignation. I held onto my rage as if it were armour. I encouraged outrage to kindle in my heart. How dare he claim to be the hands on my power? I kept myself Queen through my strength, my actions, my decisions! No man wove my destiny for me.

"Laywren," Dorn spoke firmly. "I am your servant, but not just because you lead the Horde." He stepped forward, his hand over his chest, "My heart..."

"You are not free to speak!" I said harshly, cutting off his words. "I revoke permission."

His lips pressed together, draining the blood from them. I was aware of his hand fisted at his side. We stood, locked eye-to-eye, the very air dancing between us. Then, as I hoped he would, Dorn tipped his head down. He stayed, looking at the ground, his shoulders heaving with the effort to control himself. He backed up three paces, turned and left the tent without another word.

My neck and shoulders began to ache with tension. I tried to rub out the pain, but my hands were trembling with fury. Turning, I looked at the flanks standing ready to guard me. Hinfūs was watching from the back of the empty tent, his eyes glowing in his grey face. The stillness was deafening. My vision blurred, and I blinked quickly to clear my eyes.

Never had I doubted Dorn, nor doubted his honour in his dedication to serve me. But this morning, I had seen a new Dorn—one I did not know. One I could not trust. Dorn knew I had flushed and faded, flushed and not acted. If he told the Horde of my actions against the traditions, it would be devastating to my rule. For the first time in eight years, I wondered if he would betray me.

"Left Flank." My guard stepped up to my side. "Follow him unseen."

Hinfūs was a better tracker, but the hounds were immune to Lumen's touch. I could not command or seek them with the disc.

Using Lumen, I tapped into my guard's sight, picking up the view from the flank's eyes. I could see Dorn's back moving through camp in the direction of his mount. He brushed past a Julee carrying goat water skins.

PLACING THE BRIDLE on his Alacrite mare, he flipped his cape over his shoulder and leapt onto the horse's bare back. Through the flank's eyes, I saw Dorn ride hard out of camp.

I knew I should be packing for travel, but instead I lay down and snoozed on my hides, emotionally exhausted. I tossed through strange dreams as Flank faltered and fell behind Dorn. My guard tracked the hoof marks until high sun, and finally came upon the mare, over a grassy ridge. I woke and gave Lumen's image my full attention.

Dorn had dismounted and was practicing his cut and thrust moves with his long sword. His face was grim with concentration. I watched his body turn and thrust the blade up into the ribcage of his imaginary enemy. He spun and sliced where the neck would be. His elbow bent up beside his ear, and he jabbed forward with the death strike. Dorn moved gracefully, yet with deadly purpose, his sandals stirring up the dust.

I had thought he might betray me, and yet here he was working out the anger I had seeded in him. He had not turned it on me, and not because he was weak, but because he was strong, strong enough for the both of us—strong enough to control both of us.

Sweat glistened on his muscled thighs, the sight striking a chord in my pulse. I should not have doubted Dorn's loyalty. The flush was making me weak, turning me into a spy of good men. I broke the link to Lumen, a sign for the flank to return.

The guilt at doubting Dorn's honour made me want to make things right. I thought of how I would speak to him upon his return. I would try not to mention his comment about those who kept me Queen.

I took out my goddess statue, curving my hands around her smooth sides. Holding her thus, my thoughts turned to graciousness. Truly, it was she who made me Queen. It was she who had chosen my destiny. It was she who had put Rserker and Dorn in my path so that I should be supported in all I did. It was the goddess who had granted me the power to rule.

Humbling myself, I spoke the prayer of devotion as the sun tracked across the sky outside of my tent. When my voice was harsh from overuse, I moved to return the statue to my fur pouch, when my skin caught on a sharp edge. Bringing her closer to my eyes, I ran my finger over the small, sharp foot of Goddess. I had carved her when quite young, and this was her one flaw.

WHEN I HAD BEEN 11 years old, my father had organized an Outlander journey, and I was finally old enough to be invited. Instead of making me ride my hoarge mount, father had presented me with a young Alacrite gelding. The horse had a thick, short mane and his hide was the dark brown that turns black when wet with sweat. The animal had been full of fire, dancing sideways, throwing his tail out as if ready to burst free and escape.

My mother had made me a saddle in the way of the Mantie tribe. The space between the raised horn and leather back ridge was small, only wide enough for a Mantie pelvis. It functioned to hold the rider in place during mounted two-handed combat, and it was perfect for my child-slim body.

The journey had been hard, as I knew it would be. But, this was my chance to prove myself to Outlander kin. They watched me every minute. How I rode, how I cared for my weapons, my mount, how I spoke to my father. Oh, the pride I had felt, when riding behind my father's massive, grey war horse.

After many days of traveling, we had come to a grove of Oil Berry trees. My father stopped us at a distance, so we could view the eight, great trunks. Father moved his horse close to mine. I reached out and touched the white lamb's wool hide he used to soften his saddle.

"This is the Garden of Ele-berge. Some of these trees are many thousands of years old, and from one, you shall carve your goddess *on-lícnes*," Father said to me.

That day, we camped in the shade of the Oil Berry trees. The shade was not made by the leaves which were sparse, but from the trunks that were wide enough to block the sun. While the others made camp, I visited each tree. One was an ancient stump, split down the middle and covered in warts like a boulder toad. I would have thought it dead but for six slender branches, reaching eagerly to the sky like children's arms. Another tree was circled by stones placed there by some unknown hand, hundreds of years ago. The black trunk of this tree spiraled up and split into two, its bark pock-marked. Many branches rippled from this trunk, spreading a silver canopy of minnow-shaped leaves above me. I looked carefully at each tree and tried to read their secret language in the wind's caress on the leaves.

IN THE END, I KEPT being drawn back to the old trunk, and those six reaching branches. Each branch was crowned with a small halo of leaves. This was the tree that would birth my goddess carving. I did not need a sign, for I knew it in my heart.

Climbing the trunk, I placed my sandaled feet on the raised roots, boosting myself up another foot. With a child's curiosity, I ran my fingers over the ancient bumps and grooves. *How many hands had travelled this path?* The air was warm, but the tree's bark was cool. I did not want to cut any of the slender branches, but I knew to cut the trunk would endanger the tree. I made my way around its ancient side, marveling at its girth. Twenty warriors could ring the trunk and still not reach all the way around. And then, I found it. A small knot pushing out against the tree's side, curving like a woman's hip. This was the piece that would not cut the flow of juices from the roots.

Before I raised my father's ax, I had to give respect to the Ele-berge tree. I knelt on the ground and spoke to the split side of the trunk.

> Your roots curve deep within the forest floor
> And my feet are free to walk on top
> You and I, we face the same sun.
>
> Many travelers have camped beneath your arms
> I am but a flicker in your life
> You and I, we breathe the same air.
>
> Your fruit ripens and falls in a season
> I wait many seasons to mature
> You and I, we share the same mother
>
> Please, gift me your flesh
> That I may carve her and-lícnis
> A totem through which her blessings can reach me
> A totem through which my prayers may reach her
> Great tree, I ask only this.

I took out the small axe my father had given me, and I chopped under the setting sun. With a crack, the wooden knot split from its mother and fell to the ground, rocking on its hump between my feet.

Within the hewn slivers of wood, a golden shine reflected back the sun. I knelt to examine it and found a shiny disc trapped within the piece of wood. When I rubbed the disc with my fingers, the surface lit up with light, and I felt a tugging in my mind.

"A gift from the tree," I whispered. "A gift from the goddess!"

I had bowed in thanks to the old trunk, then quickly pried out the disc with my dagger. I had felt this gift should be kept secret for the time. When I returned to my father, he saw only the piece of wood that would become my goddess image. First, I would carve my figure, then, I would explore the disc. And that is what I did, day after day, reaching into the disc's heart with my mind until we were one. Lumen became more important in my life each time I used it.

I SIGHED AT THE OLD memory and placed my goddess figure in the small pouch, settling her carefully against the fur lining. Praying to the goddess had restored my calm, and I could now consider my earlier confrontation with Dorn with a clear mind.

I had fooled myself for years. I had considered Dorn a friend, looking up to him as an advisor, while all the time, love smoldered in the ashes of my heart. The flush had forced me to consider the idea of a mate, and my spirit had secretly chosen the Chronicle Warden. And now, my feelings for him would not be subdued, could not be restrained. I could feel my need for him pulsing beneath my skin. Everything was in flux, the balance, the future, why not my feelings? Maybe Goddess had given me the flush to lead me to Dorn's side. Maybe it was time to take a man.

Hinfūs sulked at the side of the tent, glaring at me with his ears down. When I looked his way, he slunk forward on his belly.

"What is wrong, Hound?" I reached to pet his ears, but he licked at my hand, his tongue dripping with saliva. I wiped it on his neck fur, disgusted at the slimy threads.

"Out!" My mood darkened, as I chased him from the tent.

Dorn startled me as he stepped from the afternoon shadows outside.

"Would you chase me away, too?" he asked.

His tone was half teasing, and I could see he was once again the Dorn I knew. I stepped back from the entrance, inviting him in. Remembering his ride on the mare, I was surprised at his clean leather tunic, his dust-free body. I realized he had changed before returning. Any discomfort I felt about our earlier argument was cleared by Dorn's gentle smile. I willingly joined his lighter mood.

"Have you come to tell me a story?" I asked.

"If that is what you want," he said.

Together we moved further into the tent, closer to the single candle burning on the table. When we were within the circle of dim orange light, I turned to him.

"Dorn..." I started, but he interrupted me.

"Laywren, I must beg your forgiveness for the way I spoke to you."

I said nothing, standing with my hands at my sides, waiting for him to continue.

"I have waited long to tell you of my feelings, perhaps too long." He looked at me with regret. "And now the words are foreign on my tongue."

I released him from any repentance he felt he had to give. "I have never felt displeased with your service, Dorn."

He nodded and continued in his clear voice. "For eight years, you and I have complimented each other's strengths and shored up each other's weaknesses. Together, we have travelled half this world and survived what has been the end for many."

I agreed with his opinion of our relationship.

Dorn took a step toward me, smiling kindly into my eyes. "We have been blessed to have shared this time. I have been blessed to share in your life, to be by your side, to serve when you needed me, and to ob-serve when you did not."

I softened at his words.

"But now, that is no longer enough," he said, his voice low and husky.

My heart was pounding, and I knew we were coming to the mo-ment when he would say things he could never unsay. I was not sure I was ready to hear him and raised my hand as if to ward off his words.

Dorn held his tongue and ran his hand through his hair, holding the lengths back from his face as he considered me. Then, he dropped his hand and glared at some point across the tent, as if he could draw strength from the walls. Looking at Dorn's strong profile, I suddenly wished I had not stopped him. The silence between us stilled my tongue, making it impossible to speak. So, I reached out the hand that would stop his speech and touched his shoulder with it. Dorn looked at my hand, and then, lifted his eyes to my face.

"It is hard for me...," I started. It was no small thing to take down the defenses that kept me alive in this life. I had spent years building walls to ward off the simple emotions that others could enjoy freely. Others who did not have the responsibilities I had. Others who did not have to keep their minds clear to make decisions for the greater good.

I tried again, "It is hard for me, but I want to trust myself to you."

Dorn took my hand in his, holding it gently as if my sword-cal-loused hand was delicate. He slid his thumb lightly across the back of my fingers. The movement twisted his bronze wrist band, which looked dark in the candle light. Trailing vines tracked across the edges of the metal cuff—the symbol of the Eldersleen. Dorn was like the vine, reaching back into my past, and moving forward into my future. He was constant, but never binding.

"Laywren, when I saw you flush, I was elated for you. And the Horde. For all people, for your flush is the hope for life—patterns of hope brushed on skin that I have ached to brush with my fingers ..." His voice faded to a whisper on the last word.

My face burned at his words, but I hungered for his confession. I wanted to leave this moment raw—to savour it, but Dorn continued.

"But with my joy came such dread. The thought of the flush choosing a man other than me was unbearable. And the very act of thinking such a thought was a betrayal to the goddess."

I darted a look at his eyes to see if he was baiting me—if he was going to challenge me about denying Nethaz.

Instead, he only said, "Do you understand, Laywren?"

I held my breath, while Dorn waited for me to reply. I did not dare speak.

"Do you understand that what I feel for you could destroy my faith, disarm my service to the goddess, and tempt me to disregard the sacred traditions that I live to uphold?"

I had already done what Dorn struggled to resist, and he must never know I had ignored the calling to mate with the giant. Guilt made me slip my hand from his—made me want to flee the moment. A man like Dorn did not easily sacrifice his beliefs for a woman. I was unworthy of such a forfeit.

I could not even find words worthy of an answer. Reaching up, I caressed his cheek and bared my soul for his study. If he never knew how I cherished his wisdom, how I needed his words, his support, he should know now. Dorn's eyes sparkled as they explored the prospect of my gaze.

"You do see the man before you," he said warmly, and turned his head to press his lips into my hand.

His deep pleasure at discovering something that had been there all along stung me with sadness. I had pressed down my feelings until they were out of sight, out of reach. Dorn did not deserve that. He was a man who deserved more than I could give him.

"Dorn," I smiled softly, taking my hand from his face. "I do feel a kinship to you. It is more than brotherhood, stronger than warrior oaths. It is a bond that feeds my soul each time you are with me."

"But do you not want more?" he whispered fiercely, grasping my upper arms and pulling me closer to him. "Does your soul not want to *feast*, Laywren?"

Longing softened my lips and desire flashed a hot reply in his eyes. Together, we stood and breathed—the deep, rhythmic draw and release of two souls bound by the same need.

This was the moment we could never go back from—the moment when our eyes bled promises that would change our relationship forever. I was agreeable. I wanted it to change. I wanted to step into his arms and feel his body against mine. But, my legs were stiff, unbending. I could not release myself to trust him so completely. I had to bring him to me.

"I free you Dorn," I whispered.

His eyes burned bright, "In what manner, Laywren?"

"In all manners," I whispered, barely able to form the words.

He released my arms carefully, as if afraid I would change my mind if he moved too quickly. The heat from his hand burned into the small of my back as he slowly pulled me closer. I did not turn away, but I did not come easily for I could not deny this joining would change my rule, and I was not sure I could sacrifice so much. Dorn raised a brow as if he were calculating the distance between journeys.

"Why do you resist?"

Dorn's other hand wrapped my wrist, and his fingers tracked my pulse. I knew my veins throbbed with a rhythm that confessed my desire.

"Permit me, Warden, to sample this feast you claim awaits." I had meant to mock, but my words trembled in the air between us.

He shook his head at me as if I were an unruly child.

"You must accept the fire in your body before it can melt the ice in your heart," he raised my wrist to his lips, never taking his eyes from mine. "You must choose to flow with one purpose," he whispered against my skin.

The look in his eyes drained any last doubts from my mind.

"I did not know that I ached for your touch until you touched me." My voice was soft and low.

His eyes darkened with desire, the pupils shimmering with candle-light reflections. And still he waited, watching me as he touched the side of my face with his hand.

I searched for the words he needed to hear. "Long have I been yours, Dorn."

Then, I saw his love for me, and it was not the kind of love that grows in a day or a week or a year. It was imbedded in his very core, and it was hot and sharp. The bottom of my stomach dropped away, and my mouth became a beggar.

"Please, do not make me wait any longer."

Dorn choked on my name as he wrapped his hands in my hair and crushed my lips with voracity. He held me enslaved with his mouth. His warm hand slid down my back, pulling me to him, and as our bodies met, the tension drained from my body, seeping out of my pores and leaving me pliable to his lead. I clutched at his tunic with desperate hands, clinging for balance. His hand wrapped the back of my neck, steadying me, and I felt him smile against my mouth.

My vision blurred behind my lashes, and I became a speechless, thoughtless being. Fear spiked in my chest at my vulnerability, but my body was wanton, responding to instinct as the red tide of desire swept away my fears, releasing me to his embrace.

And in his embrace, in this moment; my need to rule was overcome by a hunger to be his woman.

My mind turned inward, following the burning trail of his hand on my body as he traced the curve of my hip. I wanted that hand. Wanted

it like fire wants wood. This time it was my mouth that took his, probing and biting until he pulled my knee to his hip and pushed his pelvis
against mine. My spine ground against the centre pole of the tent with
the sweet bite of awareness.

Oh yes, I thought, *Mark me here, where the serpent dared to brand
me.*

But Dorn pulled his mouth away from my bruised lips, leaving
them cold and solitary. His hand left my body to clutch the pole above
my head, and a ragged breath shuddered from his chest as he struggled
to control his passion. I tried to recapture his mouth, but he grabbed
my chin, placing his thumb against my lips. With a shaky laugh, he
leaned his forehead against mine. His hair fell like a curtain between
us, the ends flipping up to tickle my face as he spoke.

"Let us not flood love with urgency," he said.

I tipped my head back against the pole and stifled a groan. With
hands turned to supple hide, Dorn brushed the hair from my face and
tenderly kissed the base of my throat. His lips were soft and firm and
warm as he kissed my forehead, my eyelids, my cheekbones, drawing me
down from the spiraling pillar of lust into the all-encompassing cradle
of love. He pressed his lips against mine so lightly, I wasn't sure if the
kiss was real or imagined. Slowly, the pressure of his mouth increased
until my mouth parted. Many times, I had watched Dorn's lips spill
words before the fire. Now, with his gentleness, they spilled my pride.

When my knees would no longer support me, Dorn pulled me
against his chest, and wrapped me in his arms, lovingly.

"*Nú ic áh máste þearfe,*" he whispered against my hair. The words
were full of the knowing of a lover.

The tent flap caught my eye as the flanks entered. They glanced at
us, and then, moved to settle on their bedding hides. Dorn lifted his
head from mine and looked their way.

"Will their knowing turn you aside?" I asked, a grin quickening at
the corner of my mouth.

Dorn turned back to me, his words striking me silent. "Nothing will turn me from this honour," he said.

Then, he lifted me in his arms and carried me to my bed skins. Lowering me to the soft furs, he lay by my side. And I, who can wield most weapons with skill and ease, was not sure what to do. Dorn had no such hesitation. His hand touched me like silk as he slowly dragged his fingertips up the inside of my leg. I placed a hand upon his shoulder, but he winked at me, calming my nerves and his fingertips moved higher.

I started to raise my knee, and his hand changed direction. Leaning across my chest, he carefully removed my thigh dagger from its sheath. Slowly, without ever releasing me from his gaze, blade by blade, he disarmed me, passing the sharp edges over my chest to lay them beside us on the floor. When he was finished, he slipped to lie over my body, his hair touching me first.

"Let your guards count each gasp I draw from you," he said with a wicked smile.

I wrapped my arms around Dorn's neck pulling him down to me, willing to sacrifice everything for one night in his embrace.

Chapter 13: Death on the Plains

On the second day of travel, I recounted our night together. Our band was surrounded by miles of golden grasses dancing in the rare breeze. The stomp of the bullsaurs' wide feet hammered the plain as the gigantic beasts carried our possessions. All around, the sounds of adventure rose on the hot wind. Snorts from the horses and yips from the hounds were mixed with light laughter and bantering jabs from my people.

The day's heat and the rocking sway of my bullsaur lulled me into a relaxed state, and I slipped deeper into my basket to revisit my night with Dorn. My hand strayed to my stomach as I recalled his touch, for I had hopes that a seed had begun to grow.

Dorn had stayed the night with me, a night of little sleep. After he had loved me, he had propped himself up on his arm and looked down into my content face.

"Eight years I have waited for this night," he whispered, drawing his fingers down the side of my ribs.

In the past, there had been times when heated glances had passed between us, but the man of a thousand words had never spoken of his wishes. He had never stepped out of his role to court me.

"You must be a very patient man," I said with a touch of disbelief.

He laughed low in his throat. "The time spent waiting for fruit to ripen is sometimes sweeter than the harvest," he teased.

"Perhaps, I should sweeten your life with more waiting, then."

His quick glance at my eyes, left a smile twitching at the corners of my mouth.

Dorn leaned forward, tickling my nose with a light kiss. "No more time wasted, Laywren," he said.

His words sent a ripple of alarm into my stomach. Here in my tent, I could give in to his charms. But out there, beyond the private walls of my tent were the people who depended on me to lead them. I was their Queen, and I could let no man or woman distract me from that.

"There is no going back from tonight," Dorn continued, brushing my hair from my face with his gentle hand.

I felt the familiar wall rising to close off my feelings—to create a barrier between me and my emotions. I hid my eyes by catching Dorn's lips with mine.

He had been gone in the morning when I awoke, and so was the flush. That was not usual. The flush should have marked my shoulders for weeks, and I was left wondering if I had not been mistaken. Only Dorn's witness to the patterns convinced me the gift had ever graced my skin.

Reaching up with both arms, I grabbed the rough sides of the riding basket and pulled myself upright. I pulled down my woolen shift exposing my tanned shoulder to the sun's light. My skin was smooth and unmarked. Sighing, I pondered the idea that the goddess could be punishing me for not accepting Nethaz as my chosen mate. That thought left me cold with fear. I had always been in her favour, and the thought of her disfavour, and what it could bring, frightened me.

I shook off the feeling of dread. Whatever the reason, soon our travelling would be over, and I would be able to free myself from dallying over questions without answers. The current reality of the Horde's situation demanded my full attention.

A rank smell pulled me alert.

I looked to the bullsaur in front of me. The beast's huge ass swayed back and forth with each lumbering step, raising clouds of dust that threatened to choke us all. I twisted around to see past the riders at the back of the column. The path of crushed reed grass behind wound like a beige river until it dipped out of site over the hill we had crested an hour ago. To my side was another bullsaur, spread far enough from mine to leave a space for walkers in between. A hand went up in the basket, and I recognized Kaj's widow, Nailia. I nodded to her but turned my attention back to the grass.

These plains hosted badgerdoms, fierce creatures of prey that dug their way under the fields. Each year saw a loss of trees as the rains became less and without tree roots, the badgerdoms were able to tunnel freely in the soil, expanding their territory. They dug pits under the ground, pits big enough to pull down a bullsaur, and their attacks were fierce enough to kill one of our beasts. We knew badgerdom tunnels wove under the field, because the scent in the air was putrid. The wind would blow it away from us, and then change to blow it back into our path until we choked on the threat. Our great beasts snorted and tossed their huge heads, but the columns held.

The Julees herded the beasts in the shape of a V, and the lead bullsaur was in the most danger because it was breaking down the reeds blind. A few warriors walked in front, piercing the ground with their spears. But even their efforts could not detect a deeper pit that might only cave under the weight of a much larger creature. At the front of our column, a bullsaur started to sway out of line as the Julee on its back called out a command. She was rotating the animals to keep the lead bullsaur fresh. If trouble were to come from the grass, it would happen when we were making a change. I gazed into the ocean of reeds that surrounded us. The movement of the fronds was disturbing, drawing my gaze into the shifting ripples and confusing my sight.

Between the reek of the badgerdoms, the pollen from the grasses, and the dusty air, my throat became an impassible tunnel for what little spit I had left. My tongue stuck to my teeth, and Hinfūs whined as he loped beside my bullsaur. Thinking of the District well water being poisoned increased my discomfort with the heat of anger. We still had enough water for ourselves, but the bullsaurs and the hounds needed more than we had.

I recalled the mug Nethaz had spilled. The water had been necessary for the goddess' message, but so very precious to waste on dust.

The flanks did not seem affected by the heat. They rode on the other side of my beast's wide belly. They were normally quiet, but when riding, the boredom roused daggers in their speech. Lumen translated their words.

Left Flank ~ May your air be kissed by the tail's lips ~

Right Flank ~ May your grass grow beneath knee rain ~

Left Flank ~ There is a message for you between the toes of the beast ~

Right Flank ~ May you gather it for me while you crawl ~

Behind us, the food collectors hung half out of their baskets, swinging long scythe-hooks into the uncrushed reeds. I watched the lines play out across the air and then fall to disappear in the tall grass. The collectors grunted as they pulled the lines in, hand over hand dragging huge clumps of grass up into the basket where it was piled and tied. We dared not stop, but we dared never to ignore the chance to collect food for ourselves or the stock.

Suddenly, a frightened roar from the lead bullsaur shattered my thoughts. I grabbed my bow and flipped over the edge of the basket, hanging in a full stretch before I dropped to the ground. The beasts were being pulled to a stop. Warriors fell in with me from the sides, weapons drawn as the screaming din from ahead fired an urgency in our legs.

A dust cloud rose up like a wall ahead of us, and I lost sight of the lead bullsaur. I could hear the distinct growls of an attacker and the bullsaur's peals of pain. It had to be a badgerdom.

"Hold back," I put out my arms to stop my warriors from racing into the cloud of dust. Without sight, we could be shredded by the badgerdom's claws.

A figure ran out to us, staggering through the dust cloud. It was the Julee, bleeding from a wounded leg, but otherwise alive.

I ran forward and grabbed her arm, "Who rode in your basket?" I asked her.

She pushed her blonde hair back from her face and spoke through a grimace of pain, "The giant."

Nethaz! I released her, and she hobbled to another helper.

The badgerdom was thickening the dust with its assault. I could not know if Nethaz was under the bullsaur or ripped to shreds. But I did know that firing arrows into the cloud could kill him and rushing in blind would kill us.

I tapped into Lumen and sought out Nethaz's life force within the dust. He was alive and moving.

"Luchaire," I commanded Lumen.

"Find the light," I said to the warriors, and we searched the dust with our eyes until one cried out and pointed.

To the right was a ball of light and it was getting bigger.

"Do not fire upon the light. It is the giant!" I drew an arrow back in my bow and released it into the cloud to the left. There was no cry of pain, no grunt of surprise. I aimed at the middle. This time my arrow was followed by more and the volley struck a response.

"You'll hit the bullsaur!" The Julee pleaded behind us.

I turned and yelled at her, angry that she was still in danger. "Get into the basket!"

And at the second volley of arrows, the badgerdom broke from the dust cloud and raced towards us. It charged with its spiked head low hoping to impale its enemies. We split running to the sides, but the Julee could not move fast enough. She was crushed beneath its clawed paws. The beast did not pause as it ground out the Julee's life but kept on chasing those who had run to the right.

From the side, Dorn appeared, riding his mare in front of the charging beast. It turned, blinded by rage and raced after the Alacrite into the grass.

"FORM A LINE," I YELLED, and we spread out with our arrows ready. I knew Dorn would bring the badgerdom back for another pass, and we would be ready.

My eyes began to water as I focused on the grassy reeds, watching for the waves that would reveal Dorn's return. Those watching from the safety of the baskets changed their tones and this drew my eyes to them. Instead of watching for Dorn, they were peering to where the dust cloud had been. I chanced a look over my shoulder and saw the dust had settled enough to reveal Nethaz standing at the head of his fallen bullsaur. He stood crouched, his muscles bulging in anticipation, his axe shining before him. He still glowed from Lumen's light and it made him appear godlike. Members of the Horde gasped as they took in the magnificent sight. I shut Lumen down, and Nethaz's light blinked out just as the rumbling started.

I twisted my foot in the sand, steadying myself and pointed my arrow to where I thought the armoured head would break through the grass. The old man shouted from his riding basket, pointing his staff to where seconds later, Dorn burst through the high reeds on his mare. The horse's chest muscles bunched as its front hooves drove into the dust. Behind Dorn's back, the grass reeds parted in a shredding over the badgerdom's snout. The ground shook as it charged straight at us.

"Fire!" I shouted, the word not completely out of my mouth before our arrows whistled into the air and drove deep into the brown hide of the beast. It faltered but did not fall.

"Scatter!" I yelled, and we turned and ran, creating twelve targets instead of one.

I knew from the thunder beneath my feet that I was the target the beast had chosen. I threw my bow and turned for the fallen bullsaur, hoping to gain its height so I could leap onto the badgerdom's back. From my right, I saw Dorn sharply turn the Alacrite. The horse reared and then leapt forward, racing back for me.

I dug deep for the speed I needed to make the mark. Ahead, Nethaz stood watching. He straightened to his full height drawing his axe behind his head, his ribs pushing out through his chest muscles with the stretch. Then he swung forward with all his might, releasing a thunderous battle cry. The axe spun from his hands, blade over handle. I counted the turns, hoping it would find its target before the beast ran me down. When the axe would cleave me on the next spin, I changed course and dove to the side. I heard the helving of the badgerdom's skull as I tripped and rolled. The beast fell with a thunderous shake of the ground, sliding its weight along at a speed that caught me before I could regain my feet. The mound of dirt pushed up by the massive head drove me along, forcing dirt into my nostrils and half burying my torso, before the momentum stopped.

I twisted against the dirt holding me down. Dorn leapt from his horse and ran to my side. Grasping my arm, he helped pull me free from the mound. I coughed to clear my lungs and pulled away from his concern.

I turned to examine the downed beast. Dust cloaked the badgerdom, blanketing its brown fur in a reddish hue. The beast's fanged snout was buried in the ground, but the top of its armoured head rose above the dirt. Driven into the bone between its eyes was Nethaz's axe, angled as though it had been left in the chopping block.

I turned away and put one finger to the side of my nose to blow clear my nostrils of dirt.

With the dust settling, the scene was revealed to the others and a cheer went up from the Horde. Dorn and I looked at each other. I could not speak for my chest was still heaving out the dust. Dorn did not reach for me, again, but his eyes caressed me, and his lips moved over a silent prayer of thanks. I was pleased that Dorn realized I did not welcome the care he would give a woman. Perhaps our coming together would not present me as weakened to the others. I gave Dorn a small smile and nodded my thanks. Then, I moved to praise Nethaz.

The giant stood by the bullsaur, his hands at his sides. I looked up at his solemn face and this time, did not mind that he stood above me.

"I owe you a life," I said.

It was the greatest praise I could bestow. I heard the murmurs of agreement as others moved up to stand behind me.

Rserker appeared at my side. "You have proven your borh-hand, today." He smiled at the giant with pride.

But still, Nethaz did not speak. We waited patiently, wondering if he were in shock. Finally, his eyes met mine.

"It is not to me you owe the life," he said, raising his hands in front of his eyes as if to read his palms. "I was bestowed with the goddess' light."

Silence blanketed the group as those around me digested his words. Nethaz dropped his hands and looked to the badgerdom.

"It was the goddess who felled the beast!" The giant's voice boomed into the silence.

Rserker's eyes slid to mine. He knew what Lumen could do, and he had heard my command to the disc. But I did not counter the giant's words. It would do well for the Horde to believe the goddess had saved me. It would do well for all to believe we were in the goddess' favour.

Dorn moved to my side and spoke to the Horde, "We are blessed in our journey!"

Another cheer rose up. I looked to my people, pleased to see their hopeful joy.

Among the cheering and laughing of the others, one dour face stood out. One who was not hugging or shaking hands with a comrade. It was the girl—the chronicle ward. She slipped behind a group before I could be sure of her expression, but I thought she had looked my way with a hateful scowl.

Chapter 14: The Water Weirn Sacrifice

As the sun's rays lengthened, we left the plains and entered another wood. The shade in the forest was welcome, but there was no cool moisture in the air to greet us. The never-ending heat floated around the trunks, baking the leaves into orange and yellow wisps that drifted down on the windless air. Soon this forest would also collapse, and the terrain would become a new territory for the badgerdoms.

We were not a silent Horde, and the dried leaves created a crackling that would alert any enemy of our arrival. So, we stayed alert, expecting attack. I leaned against the inside of my bullsaur's basket, trying to brace a sore shoulder. Being driven into the dirt had scraped my skin, but worse, it had pained the joint. Later, I would have Hinfūs heal it, but for now I ignored the throb, and pondered Nethaz's assumption on the light. The giant was quick to believe he had been blessed. I did not know if I could fault him after the goddess' vision he had shared with me. Obviously, our oversized wúsc-bearn had a connection to the Hall that was stronger than mine. That thought pricked my pride, but only for a second. As long as the giant was a member of the Horde, sworn in loyalty to me, I could wield any power he might have.

Dorn's voice hailed me from below. I leaned over the side of the basket and looked down on his Alacrite mare, prancing gracefully to keep pace with my beast. Dorn tilted his head and smiled up at me. His presence warmed me even more than the afternoon sun, if that was possible.

"I know this place," he called.

I peeled my tongue from the roof of my mouth. "What do you know, Dorn?"

"I know there is a water weirn nearby," he grinned at me and reined in the horse as it tried to step away from the bullsaur. He had my full attention.

"Search for it," I ordered.

Dorn raced ahead on the Alacrite, moving past the front beasts who led single file through the trees. I could imagine his mind sorting through the chronicles for the right tale that would guide him to the weirn. Hopefully, the record was intact.

We travelled for four more hours, weaving in and out of the trees to find passage for the wide beasts. I did not like to think about the distance we lost on our meandering way. As the sun started to descend, we came to a clearing within the wood. The treeless area dipped down from the edge of the forest and became a valley. It was good for hiding firelight, but a bad place to be under bow fire. The hill did not entirely surround the valley for the north end opened into the forest once again. This escape route swayed my decision about setting camp. We were not easy to hide, and we had left a trail a child could follow. But, within the valley there was protection from the damaging winds, and a way out. The sides of my mouth cracked, as I gave the word to halt. I ordered watchers on the hill's edge and pacers in the forest.

While the cooks prepared the evening meal, I walked to the crest of the hill. We wouldn't set up tents, but we would build cooking fires and lay out hides around them. The outer edge of camp was ringed with the bullsaurs, horns facing out, as a first defense. I watched the great creatures lumber into position, egged on by the Julees and their sticks. Once the animals were in place, the Julees would find a tree to bury their kinswoman under.

The hounds were loping and gathering. Their desire to hunt was not driven by hunger for they had quenched themselves on the badgerdom's flesh. Its meat stunk like the tunnels it dug, so it was no good to us as a food source. Before leaving the field, the Cooks had cut off the choicest meat from the fallen bullsaur, and then we had released the hounds on the carcasses.

Four groups of warriors, bristling with spears and arrows, broke away from the Horde and moved into the forest. They would sweep for danger and take whatever game came their way. I was edgy, waiting for word of the water weirn from Dorn.

From a good vantage point on the hill, I scanned the four horizons. There was no sign of him or the Alacrite. I dared not use Lumen in case it alerted the unknown to our location. I scratched at the back of my shoulder where Hinfūs' healing still itched.

I was anxious for Dorn to find water, for nothing binds loyalty like satisfying the basic needs of a people. As we set up camp, the others spoke of the badgerdom's death and the "goddess light" bestowed on Nethaz. Such things were not soon forgotten and not easily dismissed. I stood and took one last look for the Alacrite, before walking back to camp.

IT WAS JUST AFTER DAWN when Dorn arrived. I was back on the hill, squatting beneath the protection of my cloak. Before Dorn passed the beasts, I used Lumen to gently flick his attention and then quickly shut it down. The mare turned and raced toward me. The Alacrite took the hill on diagonals, like a tacking ship. Its energy was a wonder. Dorn slid out of the saddle and landed lightly on his feet at my side. He squatted and quickly drew his cape over his head and back against the last of the night's heat.

"The wind never howls—it just pushes and burns," he said by way of greeting.

"If it howled, then it could bleed, and I would slaughter it gladly." I made my face pleasant under my cloak, though I was impatient to know what he had found.

Dorn drew his hand across his mouth to free it from dust, before taking a drink from his water flask. He offered it to me, but I shook my head, eager to hear his words. The air tried to suck the very gel from my eyes. I risked blinking my third lids under my hood.

"I have found the water weirn," Dorn said.

"Thank the goddess," I answered, "How far?"

"A half-day North West."

North West... further away from my path to the serpent. There was nothing I could do. We needed water first—vengeance second.

Dorn's face was creased with dirt-sketched lines branching out from the corners of his eyes. His lips curved at my observation.

"I did not pause to wash."

Dorn knew the thirst upon the Horde and would never put such needs first.

"Eat and then we will leave," I stood.

"No need," Dorn put his hand against the leather sporran hanging at his side, "I had pack."

RSERKER COMMANDED THE groups to break camp. The Julee's roused the beasts, driving them into a line. It took us over an hour to begin moving. The wound-hounds raced out in front, their bugling a blood-curdling sound to any within hearing.

Heading west, we crossed an open plain of lichen-covered rock. It was as if we walked on the top of a great helmet. Cook had ripped out the softer lichen and made masks that allowed some of us to breathe easier. Only those who were on foot wore them. Nine warriors loped beside the beasts. I was one of them. I tossed my cloak to the flanks, and they happily lined their basket with it.

Today, I carried my bow instead of my long sword. My shoulder was still healing and was not ready to wield my heavy blade. The bow was better, for game was always startled out of hiding by our travel. The hot air did not sear our lungs through the masks we wore over our mouths. But it pulled our sweat from our skin before our leather armour could chafe. Even an enemy could be a friend.

Dorn was mumbling on the Alacrite's back as he led our column. He was composing the chronicle, filling his mind with our journey. His ability to memorize was instinctive—each event was stored, and then later, he would weave the words into a tale of delight for the Horde.

I stopped watching him and concentrated on the pounding of my sandals, the lungful of each burning breath, the pumping of my heart. The wind picked up, and my senses sharpened until I could smell the messages on its back. My eyes stalked the sky, the ground, and my muscles were ready to defend, should we be attacked on our way to the weirn. When the way was clear, we turned our column north and continued taking the path that would present the lesser challenge.

As hunger for the mid-day meal began to build behind my ribs, Dorn pointed out the edge of a dry riverbed. Ahead, it was split by a stone and mortar dam twice the height of a man. On both sides of the dam, the river was dried out.

Dorn spoke to the Julee's who halted the beasts back from the river's edge. The warriors and I moved ahead with Dorn. They had spread out to guard against attack. With heaving chest, I stood by the bank. The jogging had winded me, even with the mask.

Moving to the dam, I took in its mechanics. On the top of the stone wall was an iron wheel. Each of the wheel's spokes had five rings and each ring was stamped with a symbol. The spokes of the wheel were like an old woman's fingers—too small for its rings.

"Do you know what to do?" I asked Dorn, as he walked past me toward the wheel.

RAISING HIS HAND, HE pointed to the right side of the dam. "The beasts must be kept from this side of the riverbed. It draws its water from the sacrifice of life. But we don't need to make one, for I know the code to open the dam and invite the water."

Dorn spoke proudly, secure in his knowledge, and in the power of his chronicles. I left him and hollered to the flanks who were still lazing in the basket. They threw down my whip. Curling my tongue, I let out a three-note whistle. Hinfūs perked his head from the pack of wound-hounds sniffing and circling near the edge of the dry bank. Then he burst from the pack and retrieved my whip.

I met him at the river bank's edge and cracked the whip's leather tail above the hounds' heads. They growled and snarled but slunk back to a safe distance. Dorn was standing by the wheel working at the mechanics with his head down. He slid the iron rings on the spokes until the places matched the ancient memory in his mind. I counted each clink but kept my attention on the hounds, cracking the whip whenever a crafty one ventured forward.

Then, Dorn called out in surprise. I twisted to see him teetering on the edge of the dam as the wheel spun and the iron plate pushed up against him. He swung his arms out to regain his balance to avoid falling into the deadly side of the riverbed. I cried out as he slipped down the side of the dam, his fingers grasping the edge as he fell. For a terrifying moment, he hung there while my heart beat three times. And then, I ran.

I cried out, dropped the whip and raced along the river bank towards Dorn. He tried to pull himself up, scrambling with his sandals against the wall. I leapt the side of the dam and ran along the top as he got his elbow over the edge and inched himself up.

Sliding the last few feet on the top of the dam, I grabbed Dorn's other wrist. Then, another pair of hands joined mine as we grabbed his elbows, then his shoulders and finally, Dorn was lying face down, gasping beside me.

"The sacrifice of my Chronicle Warden may not be worth a few drops of water," I said past the relief that made me shake.

Dorn turned to smile at me, but his expression changed to alarm at something he saw behind me. My hound's yip sounded out as I looked to see Hinfūs bounding into the deadly side of the riverbank. His great paws landed in the dry leaves that quilted the bottom. I yelled, and then Hinfūs howled, and I knew the sound of his death cry.

I raced back the way I had come, thinking I could use the whip to pull Hinfūs from the riverbed. But his body began to crumble as I made the bank. I dropped to my knees and stretched for my hound. But he was out beyond my arm's reach, and all I could do was watch as Hinfūs caved in on himself. Everything good and alive was sucked down into the dirt until all that was left were fluffs of grey fur blowing with the leaves. I burst into a hoarse scream as the lifelong connection was ripped from my insides like a gutting.

Time seemed to freeze as my cry echoed in my mind and I clawed my fingers into the riverbank.

I felt Dorn at my side before I saw him kneel beside me. "Laywren."

His voice held no compassion—only finality. His tone reflected my houndless state. Hinfūs' death was a fatal stroke, for the wound-hound was my guarantee of life. No warrior lived long without a hound. I looked up at Dorn and read the concern in his face. Behind me I could hear the murmurs of a growing crowd. I needed to stand up. I needed to look strong. What has happened is past.

Get up! Get up, damn you!

I stood, stretching to my full height before those who would see the loss as an invitation to challenge my rule. My lifeless eyes scanned the scene, taking in the stillness of my people. I saw the concern on Rserker's face as he placed his hand on the hilt of his sword. I saw old grandfather leaning on his staff, but he dropped his head before I could read his expression. I saw Nethaz slowly lower a water barrel from his broad back. And I saw the chronicle ward smirk as she stared boldly at me.

I turned back to Dorn. He did not look to me with pity. But rather bowed low. Then he straightened and spoke clearly for all to hear.

"You have saved me and as a result, you have saved the knowledge that will make the river flow," he said.

Dorn was turning this loss into a victory, once again shoring up my rule as incontestable.

"Prepare to fill the beasts," I commanded, before I walked to the crowd as firmly as I could on legs that trembled.

The warriors stood on the dry bank, looking at the riverbed where my wound-hound had been slain. They mumbled among themselves. Without Hinfūs, I would be prey to infection, disease, death by wound, and now that I was vulnerable, by challenge for leadership. All these thoughts were in their minds. I had to take control immediately. I walked straight up to the warriors and ordered them to return to their defensive positions. There was a slight hesitation. I narrowed my eyes, and then they moved.

The flanks slipped in close behind me. Their clicks had turned to hisses. Their instinct for danger was heightened, but I calmed them with a touch from Lumen. Their aggression could trigger a hostile re-action from a Horde member, and it made me look defensive. As if a battle for leadership had already begun.

The river gurgled, drawing us all away from the moment as the much-needed water began to rise on the safe side of the damn. The wel-come sound drew them out of shock and into action, and they became busy with survival.

I could relax my guard, for now.

The hounds bounded into the water, drinking and splashing. Some lay down in the water, spread-eagled to cool their bellies. They seemed to know to stay away from the dry side that had consumed Hinfūs. Dorn ordered the Julees to drive the bullsaurs to the river. Once the wa-ter was deep enough, the great creatures would dip their wide mouths into the cool river. Sucking, they would fill their second stomachs with two weeks' worth of water.

I convinced the flanks to return to our bullsaur. Then, I moved away from the group, slipping into the forest. Once in the cover of the trees, I ran, fast and silent until I was far from the Horde. I ran until my feet burned, while the sun waned, and my heart had to stop breaking to feed my blood.

STAGGERING TO THE BASE of a tree that could support my weight, I leaned on the rough bark and gagged, but there was nothing to throw up into the leaf-peppered soil. I stripped off my sandals and tied them to my belt. Then, I climbed high, digging my toes into the flaking bark. Finding a snug spot high in the forest, at the very base of a thick limb, I leaned my back against the trunk. My temples were cold with shock.

What has happened?

"What has happened?" I asked the wind.

I waited a long time for an answer.

Reaching into my fur pouch, I took out my statue of the goddess. I raised her to my forehead rubbing the wood against the beads of sweat on my face. "I devote my thoughts to you, Goddess," I whispered.

I lowered her to my breast, "I pledge my heart to you, Goddess."

I held her out, my arms straight before me. The moon shone on her rounded sides.

When had it become dark?

"I bend my will to yours, Goddess."

But did I? Hadn't I ignored her will when I had chosen Dorn over Nethaz? It was then, I saw Hinfūs' death just as the Horde members would see it—as a sign of disfavour. Only I knew what had caused the goddess' displeasure. Alone, in the tree, I began to pray for forgiveness. I begged the goddess' blessing and instruction.

"Use me as your sword. Let me strike down those who would betray you," I breathed out the words in the rhythms I had been taught as a child.

"Lead me to do your will, for my journey is in your service, and my glory is in your name."

AT SOME POINT, THE prayers and the past merged, and I was back in the Outlander village. I remembered the night the Firslain had winged down on their Griffains while we children had slept. The Guardians had delivered a special gift to the elders and a ceremony was to follow at dawn. For once, I was to be included with the other Outlander youth.

We had stood by the fence and curiously watched the adults enter the lodge used for big decisions. Little did we know then, the hound pups waited for us inside—little balls of whimpering that marked our passage from childhood to the bearing years.

Warriors needed the hound-healing the most, but females seemed to be the target of the gifts. Every family had at least one. All scrapes from childhood, stabs of the sword, even diseased limbs were healed by the hounds. My father's hound had served me well. But in my fourteenth year, the year of my first bleeding, my name was called, and I walked the length of the totem hall.

Every tribe member was there to bear witness to the ceremony, everyone, except my mother. She would not be present, because she could not be welcomed as a Mantie. I kept my head high, proud to be included, immune to the disapproving faces around me.

An Outlander elder stood at the other end of the hall, waiting to present me with my hound. Her face was as pinched as her heart against the idea of a mixed breed receiving a gift from the goddess. But the elder had no choice. The Firslain were the givers, and they chose the blessed. And I had the blood of an Outlander. I would not be denied my right.

When I stood before the woman, I tilted my head in respect as was the custom. The elder reached into a basket and lifted out the runt of the pack. Her clawed fingers shook Hinfūs roughly by his neck fur. He whined and wiggled in her grasp, pulling up his hind legs up to protect his pot belly. I smiled and reached out my slender arms, eager to hold the furry pup. But the elder leered at me and pulled a sharp dagger from her fur vest. My eyes darted into the crowd, searching for my father, and then desperately shot back to the elder, begging her not to.

She laughed, and hissed, "You shall have the pup, but not whole."

I pulled my dagger as she struck to cripple his hind leg. My blade deflected her blow. The ring of the clashing metal was followed by her harsh gasp of outrage.

"You dare strike at me, child?" The woman called out, her voice echoing through the lodge.

"You dare interfere with the goddess' blessing?" I spoke louder. My haughty pride holding me steady before the woman.

The silence was deafening. I could feel the hatred of the Outlander tribe burning into my back. They had waited long for a reason to cast me out. But a youth's heart is foolish, and I would not stand down. I would not let her maim my hound.

The elder's grey eyes glittered like flint-rock. Hinfūs had stopped whining and struggling, hanging in the air as if accepting his fate. She tossed him, skidding him across the floor, and I spun, running after. I grabbed him by the leg before he could reach the booted feet of the seated Outlanders. On my knees before the tribe, I sheathed my dagger and lifted the little pup into my arms, his hind legs kicking against my grasp. But my pleasure at his cuddle did not last.

LIFTING MY EYES, I saw my father's face. His disappointment was carved deep into his features like a stone epitaph. He lowered his head, his glance sliding from mine, and I knew the moment of his separation from me. I had shamed him more profoundly than I could know. I had broken one of the most sacred Outlander codes. I had disrespected an elder; threatened an elder... me, the half breed.

THE REMEMBERED PAIN of my father's disapproval added to the sting of losing Hinfūs, weighing down my heart until it felt as if it would slip from beneath my ribs. My arms trembled in agony as I held Goddess straight out while balancing on the limb of the tree. I had been standing thus for hours, and I welcomed the pain for it cleared my mind of memories.

A noise below curled me against the trunk in silence. A pacer walked by the tree, unaware of my presence in the branches above her.

How long before the challenges for my rule would begin?

Chapter 15: The Goddess Reveals Herself

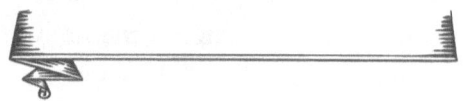

I was impatient to hunt the serpent, especially after Hinfūs' death, but I knew it would please the Horde to dally by the river. We set up our tents, mainly because I felt mine could afford me some warning of a night intruder.

Just as I expected, someone came to my tent in the night. Lying awake, I heard a whisper outside. Motioning for the flanks to open the tent flap, I silently rose, holding my daggers at the ready. A pacer stood in the full moon, her mottled skin seeming to undulate in the white light. She did not look at me, but kept her face turned down and to the side. Suspiciously, I peered into the moonlit space behind her.

"Speak," I said, when I was convinced she was alone.

She raised her glance to my chin, and whispered, "Bathes in moonlight—Goddess—along the river."

"Goddess! At the river?"

The woman nodded. My heart leapt with excitement. This would not be a trap, because pacers did not lie. But it could be a punishment from Goddess. I rushed to put on my armour. Perhaps, Goddess had answered my prayers. There was always a chance it would be a blessing. I ordered the flanks to follow, just in case.

MOVING SOUNDLESSLY through the night, we started at the riverbank, south of the dam. The air around the river was moist and cool, for the new water had quenched the soil creating a green oasis in just half a day. I marveled at the plant-life that could become lush in such a short time—proof that the world wanted to live. The riverbed wound through a dark wooded area, and we followed its snaking silver line. Wild creatures slipped back into the underbrush at our approach, reluctantly moving away from the wet shore. We walked in silence, until the forest rose up a steep incline, the trees leaning forward and falling down the slope. I could see no shoreline at the bottom of the hill, only the water and the sheer cliffs.

"Do we have to climb?" I asked the pacer.

"You follow," she said.

The woman moved into the edge of the water, stepping on stones only she knew were there. The flanks hard hooves slipped on the stones creating loud splashes, so I waved them back. The going was tedious, but soon the river turned sharply, and we came out on the other side of the hill. I stepped onto the bank's heady soil, as rich and black as night. A pungent smell of rotting wood scented the air. Ahead of me, the pacer stepped to the side, and I caught my breath as I saw Goddess in all her glory.

Rising out of the water was a fertility shrine—a tower of black hermafire-stones. Each stone was the length of four men, and each was as round as a mother's belly. The stones were too large for mortal hands to move, yet they had been laid three high on an island in the middle of the river. The moonlight seemed to pierce the hermafire's smooth sides, bending within to send silver beacons shining.

Truly, this was a sign of favour! I dropped to my knees in the newly greening moss.

"Thank you, Mother. Thank you for revealing yourself to us."

I would not make the same mistake I had made when I had awoken with the flush. This blessing was to be shared. I opened Lumen to the Horde and let them experience the wonder within my heart as it soared with renewed faith. I felt each awakening mind as my people became aware of the vision before me. Elation fed back to me through Lumen.

They would come. They would come, and we would begin the fertility rite and maybe, Goddess willing, some of us would flush.

THE SUN'S RISING FOUND most women of bearing age seated on a rock or stump along the river. We faced Goddess, together, and opened our hearts and minds to her graciousness. And we prayed. Oh, how we prayed that she would light the wick within our wombs.

As a DreÓdreng, I served Goddess in ways other than childbearing. But my union with Dorn, and my taste of the flush, had left me hoping for a babe of my own. I had no kin to prepare me for the blessing. So alone, I sat on a large rock that rested in the shallows. I dipped my shell into the river water and began combing the braids of knots that had become my hair.

I was so immersed in the task, I did not see Dorn approach until a warm hand covered mine and he said, "I would untangle such beauty."

He smiled down at me with his teasing eyes then reached out his hand for my comb like a tender. The veins stood high on the muscles of his forearm, and I felt a thrill at the memory of his distracting touch. Willingly, I released the shell to him.

We were quiet as he pulled and tugged and cut through the brambles. After releasing a difficult knot, Dorn apologized and laughingly patted my head. The motion made me think of Hinfūs. I pushed the memory down before it could score me.

A great splashing came through the shallows. Looking around Dorn's side, I saw Nethaz tromping through the calf-deep water, carrying a small wooden bowl in his large hands.

"This may soften the ties," the giant said, when he reached my side.

Unlike Dorn, Nethaz did not glow with hope. His voice was almost forlorn, and his eyes did not quite meet mine. I resisted his morose dampening of my spirits and turned to look at the wooden bowl he had brought. Sage scented goose grease whitened the bottom of the wooden dish. I nodded my thanks, and held it for Dorn to dip the comb in.

Rserker was next, bringing a garland of flowers to tie about my waist. In a land that had been parched only a day before, no flowers could have been found. But Rserker had torn strips from a piece of District cloth and had woven the pieces into flower buds. I stood to accept his gift.

"These will help you bloom," Rserker said awkwardly as he draped the wreath around my hips. I lowered my head to hide a giddy smile that rose up at the idea of Rserker crafting flowers.

"Thank you, Brother," I said, trying not to burst into laughter. Rserker beat me to it, raising his shoulders and barking out his embarrassment. I joined him gladly.

When our laughter died down, an uncomfortable silence settled. I became very aware of the water wetting my white shift and Dorn standing poised, holding the comb in midair. I looked at the giant, who looked at Rserker, who looked at the sky. Their attention was unbearable.

"Do you not have some task on shore?" I barked.

They seemed relieved as they nodded at each other and wandered back through the shallows. I snorted and sat down, shaking my head at the foolishness. Dorn steadied it with his hand.

"I think I will win this battle, if you stay still," he reprimanded.

Dorn untangled the last of the knots and my hair was released from its filthy coils. As he combed from scalp to end, the pull of the shell on my hair thrilled me.

"Now," he whispered, leaning close to my face and cradling the back of my head. "Tip."

I leaned back, arching over the smooth rock, trusting his strength to hold me. The water was cold against my head, rising with a chill to the back of my ears. Pushing his hands close to my scalp, Dorn scrubbed handfuls of sand into my hair, rubbing out months of oil and grit. My skin tingled under his fingers. I closed my eyes against the brilliance of the sun and prayed in whispers to Goddess.

> Mother, just as the buds will bloom into flowers, let me bloom inside.
> Let me be filled with nectar and sweet scents of a newborn babe.
> Mother, my fingers would touch skin that has never known air.
> My ears would hear the song of need.
> My heart would bond with another that has grown within me.
> Mother, would that I could nourish a child in my body, at my breast.
> My mind is full of all that I could share.
> I am strong, Mother.
> I am still strong, and I have guidance to give.

Hot tears pooled at the corners of my eyes as I whispered the words.

Dorn raised me up, and the tears rolled down my cheeks. I could feel his breath on my face, but I dared not look at him.

"Laywren," he rested his hands gently on my shoulders.

I peered at him through my lashes, the sun sparking the tears on my lids. Where I thought there would be pity, I found the same look of emptiness—the heartsore ache of the childless in Dorn's eyes.

"The goddess can hear your prayers, and she knows your soul," he whispered with such passion, such belief in me, I dared to believe in his words.

Dorn leaned forward and crushed my tears between our lips.

"A man's hand," said Cook, pushing Dorn to the side, "however grand."

"Cannot weave," said other Cook, coming up behind me, "we believe."

"The plait that would weight the fate!" said third Cook.

The cooks bustled between us, pushing Dorn further away from me. I smiled at Dorn's frustrated grimace as we were separated.

Accepting that he was outnumbered, Dorn stepped back, his eyes crinkling at the corners. "Very well, ladies of the pot. Braid the ladder to the Hall, and tie the knot," he bowed to them.

The three hags ignored him, as they began to pull and tug at my auburn mane, shaping it into the ancient headdress of fertility. Over their plump shoulders, and around their large ears, I watched Dorn walk down the river. He stopped to speak to each of the Horde's women, encouraging the preparations. Occasionally, he looked back at me, but I pretended not to see him.

As two yanked at my hair, third Cook lifted a skin flask and poured a bright liquid into the river. It mixed into the rippling water, swirling into the depths. Grunting, Cook leaned over her fat rolls and began making signs on the water's surface. I was taken by the graceful movements and did not notice the bright liquid rise to the top of the water until Cook scooped it into a wooden bowl.

"Drink the draught that naught could sink, and think of naught but floating kings," she said, handing me the cup.

I took the bowl, sniffing, as I raised it to my lips. It smelled of flank piss and bitterroot. How much sweeter Dorn's lips would have been. I held my breath and gulped it down. The foul liquid made me shudder and gag. The cooks laughed, pulling me upright by my hair.

"Now, now, now, now, now," they chanted with glee, draping a cloth of such vivid colour around me, I was struck dumb with wonder.

I blinked away tears of gratitude and looked for Dorn along the river. He was four groups downstream, leaning over a figure in white on a stone. The skin on my neck tightened as I recognized the chronicle ward. Dorn was tenderly washing her hair. She reached up and caressed his face. My breath came deep and low, dragged from my chest by jealousy. I wanted to use Lumen to seek their thoughts, to spy on their emotions.

Cook twisted my head to the side, forcing my gaze to the forest's edge. Among the trees, Nethaz stood in the shadows, his muscled arms crossed over his broad chest. He held my gaze, then turned and looked down the river at the object of my envy. At that moment, I hated the giant for witnessing my weakness.

A LARGE TENT WAS RAISED on the river's shore, and as dusk approached, we women were moved into its warm embrace. Not one of the others sat until I had chosen my place. Then they settled. The women admired each other's hair and adornments, petting with compliments and giggles. I hardened myself to their flattery as they praised my Hall ladder and eventually, they moved away to chatter among themselves.

"Many times, have I been overlooked by Goddess," a woman said as she knelt beside me.

"May Goddess see you first, this day," I replied, recognizing the woman as Kaj's widow, Nailia.

"No woman can compete with the presence of a Queen," she answered, her voice smooth on the compliment.

I searched her sun-browned face but found only sincere admiration.

"Maybe not a woman, but what of a girl?" I asked, nodding toward the chronicle ward, who seemed to be the darling of the others.

"Not such a girl. She buds beneath her shift, and her eyes are cunning with tainted plots," Nailia whispered.

I considered her accusation for it supported what I had seen of the girl's actions. She was seemingly sweet on the outside, but she hid a shrewdness beneath her youthful beauty.

The cooks entered the tent carrying a heavy, fire grate. I had never seen it before and was taken with the intertwining pattern of the cycle worked into the iron. But even more distracting were the green masks the cooks were wearing. Everything had become ceremony, down to the swish of their grass woven clothing.

COOKS LAID THE GRATE in the middle of the tent. Then, they filled it with sage leaves, trout-wood twigs and glittering bits of the mountains. Stretching out their puffy, white arms, they held hands around the grate. Moving in step, they circled it, chanting together.

May the moon lead the way
with beams to sway
the blessings of Goddess.
Might the stars light the flight
of the babies' souls, tonight
with the blessings of Goddess.

They sang their chant over and over until a small spark smoldered in the trout-wood. It wiggled like a glow worm among the leaf litter before it touched the mountain shavings. Then light burst upon the walls, blinding me. Instinctively, I leapt to my feet, putting my hands out to protect myself. As I blinked away the flash, a figure slowly focused in front of me. It was the chronicle ward, scorn staining her face. I blinked again, and she was back at the wall surrounded by her swarm. My hands felt empty without my sword.

"Clear your mind of all but a mother's love," whispered Nailia.

She sat down and patted the ground beside her. Then, she lay back and closed her eyes, crushing her short, spiked hair against the ground. The widow was right. The goddess would not choose an unfit to fill. I breathed out deeply, settling again beside Nailia. Closing my eyes, I tried to trust, but could not stop looking through my lashes to see where the ward was. She was on her back, rubbing her stomach in smooth circles, singing a child's lulling song.

"Mother," I began to whisper, but Cook came to touch my skin.

The old crones were circling the women like vultures, looking for signs of the flush. I could hear the murmur of the men talking quietly outside, as they waited by their fires.

Would Goddess bless me twice? Would she bestow the flush on me, when she had already tested me, and I had failed?

I tried to pray again, "Mother...,"

Maybe the flush had been enough, and I was already with child—with Dorn's child. I smiled and placed my hands on my birth-knot. I could use Lumen to sense if a child grew within me, but it might be dangerous to seek a developing mind.

Nailia's prayer pulled me from my imaginings. "Mother, bless me, for I am good. I am your obedient daughter. My body is your vessel, the pod prepared for your blessing. I live only to serve as MÓdere to your child. Let me carry your babe. Let me raise your child to know your ways, to serve you."

I turned away but continued listening. Perhaps, I should repeat her prayer. But I could not say those words. Mine were different. I served in higher ways then just being a vessel. I was the right arm of Goddess. I fed the cycle, so that MÓderes could fulfill their destiny.

Ungracious thoughts, I reminded myself.

To clear my mind, I pictured the water by the rock. But soon, I began to recall Dorn's touch as he washed my hair. The night we had spent together, Dorn had touched me like no man had ever dared, pulling me into his arms, pressing me down with his weight. His mouth had travelled my length, nipping and licking and kissing until all my will was consumed. I had been eager to surrender—weak, yes, but so very willing. I believed it was safe to give myself to him, to trust him. And he had looked deep, had done his own seeking to find my devotion.

"The greatest gift from a warrior Queen," he had whispered.

IN MY MIND, THE MALE captive's green eyes replaced Dorn's, and I felt the heat of vengeance fire my chest. I had to slay the serpent to purge it from my memory. I envisioned the male captive, with his thick, tattooed lips and the slack skin around his jaw. How easy it would be to skin that man with my dagger.

"My Queen!" Nailia whispered, disapprovingly.

I opened my eyes and looked at her. She was lying on her side facing me, her head pillowed in her hand.

"Your thoughts are not of mothering," she winked at me with a smirk.

I was taken aback, uncomfortable with her friendly liberty.

"My thoughts are for the Horde and its survival," I replied turning onto my back to look at the top of the tent.

"You have much on your mind," Nailia agreed and rolled onto her back. "And I'm sure many are thinking of you."

I sighed and sat up. She was not going to let me be.

"Say what you mean, widow," I whispered, harshly.

Nailia smiled, bringing my attention to a scar that ran across her lips.

"I saw the gifts bestowed upon you at the river's edge," she waggled her eyebrows at me.

I frowned threateningly, but her black eyes twinkled without fear.

"You have many champions, all sturdy men who could father a babe."

I ignored her teasing and looked around. The other women were focused on gentle, nurturing thoughts, and I was filling my mind with this foolishness!

Her whisper came at my elbow, "I bet the giant could fill a woman to satisfaction, eh?"

"Be still," I warned her.

But her comment led me down another path of wondering. Angrily, I pinched the inside of my arm to clear out any thoughts of Nethaz and his size. I dug out my goddess carving, turning my back to Nailia's eyes.

"Mother, I have lost my way. I am sliding between the rings of the cycle. I would hold a sword in my right hand, and a babe in my left. My heart yearns for a man to sire my child, but my mind covets the control of an army. No daughter can be both MÓdere and DreÓdreng," I stated the obvious.

Holding my goddess carving to my cheek, I whispered, "Mother, please help me find my way."

"And that General of yours," Nailia breathed out the words. "What woman would not want to warm herself in his hides?"

I turned to look more closely at my companion. She laughed softly at my discomfort. I calmed myself, trying to be tolerant—accepting like a mother would be. I noticed her scarred lip again and changed the subject from Rserker.

"Nailia, why was your mouth not hound-healed?"

She put her fingers to her lips, and I saw them tremble.

"Because Kaj decided that I should be marked," she said.

I had never heard of one withholding the hound's healing. The thought disturbed me.

"Then it is good I have killed Kaj," I said, without looking at her mouth.

"Think only of a Mother's love," she shushed me.

Chapter 16: Blessing by the River

"The flush," screeched Cook, "we have been blessed!"

I awoke with a start and looked around the tent. Women were leaping up and crying out "Who?" "Who is blessed?" "Who is it?"

I grabbed Cook's arm. "Who has the flush?" I growled, shocking even myself with my ungracious tone.

"One who has sung of others, but who will now be the song." Cook rushed off, pleased with herself.

I heard the men's voices rise with excitement outside. They had stayed awake all night, waiting for this moment. My eyes focused in the dim light, and then I saw her. The chronicle ward stood at the other side of the tent with her head held high, looking straight at me. She was surrounded by women kneeling at her feet, stroking her legs—praising her fortune. I saw the bright red swirls at the base of her neck—the sign of her readiness. My heart ached with loss, but I pushed away the pain and approached her.

"You honour the Horde with your blessing," I said.

"I thank the goddess for the honour," she replied. The words were right, but the way she held her head belied humility.

I swallowed against the bitterness in my throat. Nailia moved to my side and provided the next line that I should have spoken.

"Goddess has chosen well," said Nailia.

"And *I* will choose well," the chronicle ward whispered, never dropping her gaze from mine.

"Come!" shrieked Cook, holding the tent open for me to announce the girl.

I carried the ward's triumphant stare with me like a shadow into the morning's light. When I stepped from the tent, I was met with the anxious faces of the men. They stood as one, in silence.

I opened my mouth to speak but was struck by their faces turning to gold under the sun's rays. I turned from their gaping mouths to the river behind me to see the sun peeking from behind the hermafire stones. An aura lit the stone curves sending dancing yellow glitters across the rippling blue water. I felt the grace blossom in my heart as I heard it ripple through the men. Such unnatural splendor could only be bestowed by Goddess. Struck by shame at my selfishness, I dropped to my knees and the Horde knelt with me.

"GODDESS, YOU ARE GRACIOUS. We have waited many years to receive your gift. Our hearts are filled with joy, our minds are filled with wisdom, and all for the child you would bestow upon us. Your name shall grace our lips with glory, and we will hold your child high for all to see—a sign of the wellbeing of the cycle," I prayed.

We rose as one and witnessed the chronicle ward enter the light. The dawn lit the red swirls at the sides of her neck, and a low moan went through the Horde. Some had never seen the flush. I had never seen it like this. Her markings were like welts of blood rising along her white skin. Now I knew that my markings had been pale ghosts of the sign.

The men of the Horde quickly spread out in a line facing the chronicle ward. Each waited eagerly with the hope of being chosen. In earlier times, young men would have been standing for the choosing, but after years of barrenness, the Horde had only middle-aged men to offer the young woman.

I felt Nethaz move to stand behind me.

"Do you not stand to be selected?" I asked him.

He looked down at me and smiled softly, "I have already been chosen".

I turned away, mortified that he knew my flush had chosen him. But of course, he would have known for he had seeked my mind, as I had seeked his with Lumen.

The chronicle ward walked slowly to the line of men, basking in her day of glory. They were quiet and still, not their usual boastful selves. Pausing in front of each man, she displayed careful consideration before moving to the next. Before her contemplation, some stood tall and strong, others squirmed. Her display was puzzling to me, for I knew how strong the choosing would be, and I knew it would have nothing to do with her will.

Even Rserker contained himself as the girl stood before him. She touched her finger to her lip, looked him up and down, then passed him by. Rserker dropped his chin to his chest.

I had not thought of Rserker as a father. To me, he existed only as a warrior, as a brother—to carry out my commands. Yet, my father had been a vigorous warrior like Rserker. I was suddenly surprised to find they were comparable.

My concentration was drawn back to the ritual of choosing as the chronicle ward approached Dorn. I examined him as she would, my eyes running over the smooth muscles of his arms and legs, the straight back. His golden brown eyes were smoked by lush, dark lashes, but it was the knowledge behind them that struck a fire in my chest. I caressed the waves in his hair with my eyes. I knew he wanted to be a father; they all did. Dorn looked down on the girl with a Warden's care.

Then, Cook clapped her hands in glee, as the chronicle ward reached out her hand to Dorn.

"The flush has chosen!" Cook shrieked.

A cry went up among my people.

Dorn reached out and took the girl's fine-boned hand in his.

I held my face like stone, overriding the emotions trying to escape. Thankfully, all eyes were on Dorn and the girl as the group congratulated them. I prayed in silence for strength, trying not to leap across the moss and drive my dagger into her heart. The heat of Nethaz's hand wrapped my shoulder and grounded me.

His deep voice rumbled in my chest, "No man can refuse the call, once he has become aware of it."

The words were not meant to comfort me. The giant was reminding me that I had denied him the right to accept. Worse, I had risked the goddess' disapproval because of my feelings for Dorn.

How stupid that seemed, now! How foolish to risk all for a man!

I shook off the giant's hand and hissed at a pacer who was standing nearby, "Fetch me the skin-writer!"

I did not follow the others as they danced and sang Dorn and the girl back to camp. Instead, I walked to the rock on which I had garlanded myself for the blessing. Standing behind the grey boulder, I faced Goddess, my heart hardening into my own version of hermafire stone.

The choosing was a tradition as old as life itself, and I had been wrong to deny tradition its right.

"I accept the role of DreÓdreng as my destiny," I called out across the river.

My voice echoed in the morning river-mist, but there was no reply. Roughly, I untwined the Hall ladder, releasing my auburn hair to fall to the middle of my back. Then I dug my fingers into my skull and pulled my hair back into a fierce battle bow, stabbing it into place with sharp twigs that had tried to bob past on the river's surface. As I jabbed in the last stick, I heard the frantic splashing of the skin-writer approaching.

"What will it be, my Queen?" he asked breathlessly, his pigeon chest laboring with the effort to get enough air.

I turned my eyes back to Goddess—now a black silhouette against the red ball of the rising sun. With rough hands, I ripped my gown from neck to belly, dropping it to float around my hips.

I answered the puffing man without looking at him, "You will cloak my back with the war-dragon."

I PAUSED AND ENVISIONED Dorn reaching his hand out to the ward.

"May it eternally thrust me into battle in the service of the goddess."

Bracing my hands on the stone, I leaned over, eagerly anticipating the distracting jab of the writer's ink-blade.

Every stab to my skin pinched the arousing, parasitic emotion out, killing my love for Dorn and strengthening me to my former glory as a leader of warriors. I released my third eyelids to keep my eyes moist as I held my unblinking stare on the hermafire stones.

Before me, the rising sun turned the colour of the river to blood.

"And blood you shall have," I promised.

The End

wes thu hal -
be whole and
hearty

DEAR READER,

If you enjoyed my book, please show your appreciation by leaving reviews at Goodreads and Amazon.

Scroll down for a free chapter of Book II as Laywren's story continues.

Kind regards,

Cheryl

Continue Laywren's story with Book II of The Precious Quest
http://www.cherylcowtan.com

Read chapter 1 of Book II below.

Book II Chapter 1: The Brownie Bones Foretold

Though we had finally found a paradise of water and game, for two days I burned with frustration, blood lust, and jealousy. My lover, Dorn, and the girl chosen to be his flush-mate by the Goddess did not leave their tent over that time. Worse, the warriors who were tracking the escaped serpent had not been able to rediscover the lost trail at the base of the mountain. I wanted nothing more than to ride for the mount's base, hunt and slay the beast, but I was forbidden by tradition to interrupt the joining of the chosen. I had to wait the allotted time for the flush-mates to come together. Only when it was certain Dorn's seed was planted deep in the girl's belly could I ensure my sword would be planted deep in the serpent.

To survive the spell, I filled my mind with the serpent's invasion of my body, reliving it, questioning what it had done to my insides, wondering if it had cooled my flush and returned me to a barrenness that mirrored our world, the land, and the Hall of Return from which no souls came home. The thoughts goaded my anger.

When my rage ran so hot, I thought it would light fire to the dry plains, I channeled it into my weapon. Leaning over my blade and dragging the whetstone over the blade pulled my new inking tightly over my spine. The war-dragon tattoo itched and burned across my back. I reveled in the pain for it urged me to take revenge on the captive who had shed his skin in my tent and slithered away from my clutches.

When I could sharpen the steel no more, I sought a diversion that would slake my war-lust. Moving in the opposite direction of Dorn's tent, I walked briskly, intent on running through the unbearable heat to the ridge of sand shielding our encampment. But as I passed one of my warrior's tents, spoken words slipped from inside and stilled my legs.

Pausing, I leaned closer to the brown hide wondering what "was lost" to the one who had spoken. Did they speak of my faith in the goddess? My ability to rule the Horde? My body which could no longer be healed by my wound-hound, Hinfūs who was lying dead in the riverbed? Or were we all "lost" in this world of billowing, red sand that blew away from the roots of the last remaining trees with each gust of blistering wind?

The sound of women laughing flowed from within the skins and though I had believed brutal, physical punishment would ease my mind, the joyful cadence of their speech drew me forward.

From without, I stated that I would enter.

The tender, Eavlyn, who had been captured from the District we had last conquered, opened the flap and bowed. I had gifted her to Jendara, a warrior I had had little personal contact with. As I passed into the soft light the sun created on the well scraped hide-walls, I nodded first at Jendara, and then Nailia. The women were seated on cushions before two mugs on a small table. I had not seen Nailia since the choosing, and I was not sure I wanted to see her now.

Jendara stood abruptly in a swift, fluid motion. With a smile of welcome, Nailia brushed her veil-like skirts down as she stood. The layered material cascaded to drape her shapely legs. She stood by Jendara, her proud head held high, and her inner fervor so bright one would think she were the sword wielder.

It was not my way to visit my people inside their living spaces, and I was unsure as how to proceed. Jendara's head was down, a question hanging in the air as she waited for my orders.

"I would see more of the tender's weavings," I said by way of excuse.

The discomfort lifted.

"Of course, Queen Laywren." Jendara clapped her hands at Eavlyn, but she need not have. The woman was already scrambling through a trunk of clothes.

"Come, sit here, my Queen." Nailia smiled and fluffed a third cushion, then placed it on the floor beside her.

I looked to Jendara, for it was her dwelling. She gave a slight nod, her eyes sliding away from mine as a flush stained her cheeks. Following courtesy, I slid my sword out of its sheath and laid it against the tent wall, then moved to the women. I slowly lowered myself to the floor.

A few days earlier, when Nailia and I had been in the flushing-tent together, I had practiced a rare camaraderie with her. The woman was unafraid of my status, skirting the edges of disrespect through her affectionate, if bold comments. She was much like my general, Rserker. Much like, but different because she was a woman. Most women were subservient in my presence, some were envious, and few were friends.

Not wishing to be revered, I freed them from formality with a wave of my hand.

"What is it I have broken up with my presence?"

"We were having a game," Nailia grinned. "And we would like to continue it."

I slid my eyes to my warrior, but Jendara ducked her head to avoid my gaze. Taking a deep breath, I tried to accustom myself to Nailia's boldness.

"What is the game?" I asked.

By way of answer, Nailia shook her hand and scattered small pieces of brownie carcass onto the table.

It was clear the women had been future-reading with truth-or-tale, telling bones. Cook was the one who usually relayed our paths, but I knew others dabbled in these magicks, and I had not forbidden it.

Eavlyn, seeing my interest in the bones, put away her weavings and brought another mug. I took it from her hand before she could set it on the scattering of ribs.

"What answer do you seek?"

Nailia leaned over and whispered, "Who next will be blessed by the flush!"

I looked at Jendara, who this time was able to hold my stare. Nailia began separating the bone fragments with her slim fingers.

When we had taken the District, we had found a young woman, younger than any in the Horde. Dorn had deemed her a Chronicle Ward, but more valuable to us, she had been the first woman to flush with fertility. Not just the first in the Horde, but everywhere we had travelled. Every village and tribe we had conquered over the past nineteen years was without children.

So, she was the first, except for me. Only Dorn and the giant, Nethaz, knew I had flushed and faded. Dorn, the keeper of our legends was the man I had wanted to mate. But Nethaz was the mate the flush had chosen for me. I defied tradition. I chose poorly. And so, my chance to be MÓdor dissolved, and the Chronicle Ward's began.

Lost in my regrets, I watched Nailia place the tiny brownie ribs and rosined fairy wings into two separate stacks, the legs and arms into another. As she sorted, she was careful not to change the direction in which they had landed.

I had never considered the Horde would be blessed with another flushing after my fade. I had not though it possible to be gifted with two in as many days. But why not more?

I gulped the tea to wet my suddenly parched throat.

"To help the brownies tell their tale...," Nailia said, taking out her dagger, "We need to spill three pools of blood."

Nailia held the dagger's horn handle so tightly her knuckles whitened. The tender was hovering but stepped back when I looked her way.

I was keenly aware of my sword leaning against the far wall of the tent.

Nailia motioned to Jendara with the blade. Reluctantly, the young warrior stretched out her hand. Nailia clasped her fingers and pulled Jendara's arm closer. With the dagger's point, she made a small slice in Jendara's inner wrist.

As soon as the cut was made, Jendara's wound hound rose up from the corner of the tent and began to whine. The tender grabbed the hound by its neck fur, holding it back from the healing.

A pang in my chest roused as I thought of mine own hound, Hinfūs. Grief made the sides of my mouth heavy.

What is done is past. Look to what is coming.

I focused on the drop of ruby-coloured blood welling up from the cut. Nailia gave it a cruel squeeze, and the blood rolled over her broken nail and dripped onto the table.

"Hm," I grunted and gulped more tea.

Nailia poked her own wrist with the dagger and squeezed out another pool of blood. She was careful not to mix her life juice with Jendara's.

My mind leapt to Dorn and his ward and what they might be doing together. Memories of his body next to mine gave me much to ponder.

"Shall we add a little more?" Nailia asked, as she held out her hand for mine.

The war dragon simmered like midnight coals on my back, incensed by the thought of Dorn and the District girl sharing the love that should have been mine.

My nostrils flared, as I glared darkly into Nailia's glittering, sly eyes. "More of your blood?" I growled.

The tender moved as if to fetch something, then stopped. Jendara sat back, her hand not daring to slip to her own short blade.

Nailia broke the tension with a smirk. "We have *just* enough."

She laid the dagger on the table closest to me. Then turned her attention to the pile of yellowing bones.

Jendara released a long, slow breath.

I tipped the mug up to my lips, then paused with the liquid touching my lips as I watched the bones shiver. Carefully, placing the mug down, I looked closer at the pile in the middle of the table. Between the stacks of parts, the two pools of blood glistened. But when I turned my head to the side, the bone piles shifted and seemed to be within the blood drops.

"Now, we will chant." Nailia reached out for my hand.

When I didn't give it, she explained. "We all all have to chant if we want to find out the answer to our query."

Jendara joined hands with Nailia but she did not reach for mine. I hesitated, sniffing loudly to clear my nose. Nailia was not lowering her hand. She had much courage in the face of my scowl. I reached out my right hand and clasped hers, giving her knuckles an extra squeeze as punishment for her insolence. Without looking at Jendara, I reached out my other hand. She took it. Eavlyn watched nervously from the trunk.

"Brownie ribs and fairy wings," Nailia started. "Don't build fibs with webbing strings."

Jendara joined in the next line, her voice strangely trembling. "Answer us true, when we ask. Dance the bones, fulfill your task."

The women repeated the chant. I chided in my mind, for the game was foolish time spent, and I was becoming uncomfortably aware of the moistness in Jendara's palm. Yet, I didn't get up and leave. In a small way, I was intrigued by this distraction.

"Brownie ribs and fairy wings,
Don't build fibs with webbing strings,
Answer us true, when we ask,
Dance the bones, fulfill your task."

Just when I was wondering how I could sip another drink of tea with my hands trapped, the women stopped chanting.

Without breaking our circle, Nailia leaned over the bones and hissed, "Who shall be next to flush?" Her voice screeched on the last word, sounding like one of the Cooks casting a spell.

We held completely still, waiting for the answer to boom from above, or rise from below, or blow in through the tent opening. But as time moved on, there was nothing but silence, and my growing awareness of discomfort. Jendara was holding my hand with all the pressure of a wet leaf. I let go, dropping her hand into her lap. She would not meet my eyes. Nailia was harder to release, for she hung on while she stared down at the brittle bones on the table.

"Tell us!" she shouted, rippling the small circle of blood with her breath.

Jendara reddened at Nailia's desperate tone.

I had not realized Nailia cared much about the flush. I had been so absorbed in myself during the night of the choosing, I had not thought of her needs. Now I could see the fine lines around her eyes—signs of her aging. Like me, and Jendara, and the tender, she was barren and only getting older.

I stopped trying to pull my hand from hers and instead, gripped back. "Perhaps the brownie needs another drink?" I asked to soften her disappointment.

Jendara waved at the tender who rushed to fill our mugs. My vision shifted again as I turned to the side. I was sure the tea was drugged, but only for pleasure, not harm.

Nailia straightened and released my hand. Gripping her hair by the roots, she made the short, black spikes stand straight up between her clenched fingers. I thought she might shriek, but instead she laughed softly.

"Bare-bones brownie," she said to the pile. "Still mad at me for skinning you, eh?"

Jendara snorted into her tea. I looked at Nailia with approval. It was not easy to catch a brownie. The little people were vicious and could blink in and out of our realm effortlessly to avoid capture. To fail to catch one could bring on a plague of revenge.

Thinking of Brownies made my skin crawl and I quickly scanned the edges of the tent for darting shadows.

Continue Laywren's story with Book II of The Precious Quest
http://www.cherylcowtan.com

Image Copyright

canstockphoto674591 The Precious Quest WoundHounds Can Stock Photo oscarcwilliams.jpg

canstockphoto3580034 The Precious Quest Can Stock Photo rolfimages Hall of Return.jpg

canstockphoto8341309 village huts The Precious Quest Can Stock Photo Inc. frankix.jpg

canstockphoto8664859 war dragon the precious quest Can Stock Photo MisterElements.jpg

canstockphoto9251587 captive snake woman The Precious Quest Can Stock Photo Inc. Fotolit.jpg

canstockphoto11576730 Precious Quest Can Stock Photo curaphotography Nethaz Giant .jpg

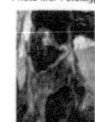

canstockphoto18466247 The serpent in the Precious Quest Can Stock Photo Inc. konradbak.jpg

canstockphoto18817391.jpg

canstockphoto19426644 Dorn The Precious Quest Can Stock Photo Inc. prometeus.jpg

canstockphoto27525727.jpg

canstockphoto37055560 The precious Quest Can Stock Photo Inc. Fotolit.jpg

Dam Rusty Valve Wheel Canva Precious Quest.jpg

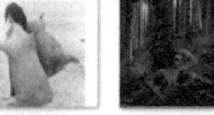

desert dryness canva precious quest.png

District Girl Canva Precious Quest.png

goat water skin canva precious quest.png

Goddess tree.png

laywren warrior or mother precious quest.png

Laywrens father Canva Precious Quest.png

man on alacrite in desert Canva Precious Quest.png

snake man Canva Precious Quest.png

three witches Canva precious Quest.png

Warrior Horde Canva Precious Quest.png

Don't miss out!

Visit the website below and you can sign up to receive emails whenever Cheryl R Cowtan publishes a new book. There's no charge and no obligation.

https://books2read.com/r/B-A-QHOD-IVGL

BOOKS 2 READ

Connecting independent readers to independent writers.

Also by Cheryl R Cowtan

The Fergus She
Girl Desecrated: Vampires, Asylums and Highlanders 1984

The Precious Quest
The Precious Quest: An Epic Journey of Love, Identity and Power
The Precious Quest II: An Epic Fantasy of Love, Faith and Redemption

Watch for more at www.cherylcowtan.com.

About the Author

Cheryl R Cowtan is an award-winning educator and fantasy author who loves to write on the wild side, digging deep into those unspoken secrets of society's seedier sins. If you love suspenseful, edgy fantasy that digs up the unspeakable, then Cowtan is the author for you. Her novels won't leave you morose, but they will make you think about a lot of things, things better left buried... forgotten. Did you know some people strip the flesh from Brownie bones and use them to tell the future? Did you know there are descendants of the Salem witches still practicing dark vengeance? Did you know... Well, maybe you should just go find out for yourself. http://www.cherylcowtan.com Warning, though... once you start reading her books, you might not be able to stop.

Read more at www.cherylcowtan.com.

www.ingramcontent.com/pod-product-compliance
Lightning Source LLC
Chambersburg PA
CBHW021041130626
46552CB00005B/1960